Home for Christmas

D. P. Conway

Part of the
Christmas Collection

Day Lights Publishing House, Inc.
Cleveland Ohio

From Darkness to Light through the Power of Story

The Christmas Collection

Go to Series Page on Amazon

or

Search DP Conway Books

Did you receive this as a gift? Please post a review on
AmazonYou can reach Dan at authordpconway@gmail.com

Dedications

For Marisa
Thanks for allowing me to follow my passion.

For my biggest fans, my children,
Colleen, Bridget, Patrick, and Christopher.

For my future biggest fans,
my little Aubrey and my little Avery.

For Colleen, whose genius was invaluable to this story.

Contents

Sunday

Jake slowly turned his rickety blue 1966 Chevy Impala, with 103,000 miles on it, off the state route and onto the quiet main road that led into the small city of Sandusky, located on the shores of Lake Erie in northern Ohio. Snow was coming down hard, and the streets were well-covered, barely visible.

It was Sunday night and only a week before Christmas. 1970 was quickly coming to a close, but Jake wished it would end even sooner. The trip up from Louisville had taken twice as long as it should have. Blowing snow and icy rain had followed him from the start.

He finished his beer and tossed the bottle onto the back floorboard, listening to the hollow clang as it settled in with the other bottles. He was chilled, as he had turned off his heat a half hour earlier, thinking it might help him conserve gas. Up ahead, he saw what looked a gas station sign, and he was hopeful…but no sooner did he realize that the gas station's lights were off.

"Dammit," he said, glancing down at his gas gauge. He did not swear often, only when he was drunk—and right now, he was that, as well as very tired and very frustrated.

The main street looked desolate on this wintry night. Businesses were closed, but lights could be seen upstairs, where people lived above their stores. He turned onto E. Water Street. Again, no lit signs, just two-story shops, all closed, with warm lights shining out from the upstairs of a few, though most were in complete darkness. Jake squinted and wiped the windshield. In the distance, he could see a diner light flickering, but as he approached, he realized the business was closed.

The snow was picking up now, hitting his windshield faster as his wipers struggled to keep up.

He glanced down at his gas gauge again, whispering a prayer of desperation. "God, help me to find a gas station." He felt funny asking God for help, especially while drunk, but the lines of what was proper and not proper always blurred for Jake when he was drinking.

Up ahead, he saw the glow of a store window and exhaled a deep sigh. Something was open. He turned the wheel slightly, crunching the untarnished snow, and peered through the windshield wipers. The snow was coming down heavily, but he could read the dimly lit sign. It was white, in the shape of an oval, with bold maroon letters and a lone light shining down on the wording: VOLSTEAD BAR AND INN. In italics under the name it said, *A Speak Easy Bar.*

"Speak easy?" Jake mumbled. "Speak easy to who?" His brow furrowed, and his alcohol-induced frown deepened. "I wish my wife would speak easy!" Jake reached into his coat pocket and pulled out the letter she had left for him before leaving for work yesterday.

Jake,

We have argued for too long. I am done talking. I have made decisions, and I am putting them into a letter in hopes you will finally get it. We got another letter from the IRS today. It says you now owe $11,000. I know I told you to leave so I could have some time to think, but I have made up my mind. I'm through, Jake. Your drinking, you're not working...you've let yourself go. We owe the IRS $11,000! I can't take it anymore! It's over.

We need to separate. I don't want you to come back. You need to move out, now.

I'm sorry. I have tried everything. You just don't get it. Jake...I hope you find happiness, but I am afraid it won't be with me. And please, for your own sake, get help with your drinking problem.

Goodbye,
Myrna

Jake shouted at the page, "I'm not an alcoholic!" Jake knew he was not. He drank because it hurt too much. His failures, his lack of direction. It all depressed him. Drinking was the only way he could mask the pain of his life.

He covered his face with one hand, wincing, feeling numb from his head to his feet. Reading her letter late last night had thrown him over the edge. Despite being hungover, he got up early, packed his bags, and headed here, to Sandusky. It was his last hope.

He slumped down in his seat, staring at the words. *Goodbye.* She really meant it this time. She had been telling him they needed to separate for six months, but now, writing it all down and leaving the letter for him on the counter... It was for real. It was over.

He carefully folded up the letter, wishing to preserve it for reasons he could not understand, and placed it into his pocket. He then looked over at the lights coming from inside the bar. He reached across the seat and cranked the window handle, rolling down the passenger window to get a better look inside. A tall bartender with sprinkled black and gray hair, wearing a baseball cap, was laughing with a lone patron, an equally older man sitting on the barstool, his hand gripping a glass of beer.

Jake looked out at the desolate street. There were no gas stations, to be sure, nor anything else open. He sighed. He was feeling buzzed and tired and did not feel like talking to anyone. But he was running out of options. He looked inside again—the bartender and patron were looking out at his car.

Jake pulled closer to the curb, turned off his engine, and reached across to roll the window back up. He got out and hustled through the deepening snow to the old wooden door with the SCHLITZ BEER sign illuminated on it. When he pulled open the door he was hit by a wave of very warm air, coupled with the scent of clean but old wood and carpet. The place was expansive and felt empty. There was a long bar that could hold perhaps fifteen people. High-top wooden tables with old wooden chairs dotted a wide-open old wooden floor. On the far end of the room, a wooden staircase ascended to some type of upstairs. Jake figured that must have been where the rooms for the inn were. The whole place seemed lost in time. Although it was 1970, in here it looked more like the 1920s.

"Hello, stranger," the bartender said in a friendly voice. The patron nodded in accompaniment. The bartender was of medium height and looked to be about fifty. He had gray speckles in his short brown hair. His eyes were large and brown, and his entire face offered a feeling of kindness.

"Hi," Jake said timidly.

"It's a cold night to be out," said the bartender.

"Yeah…I got caught in the storm," Jake said, slowly.

"Where are you headed?" the bartender asked, flipping the bill of his baseball cap from back to front.

"Here, to Sandusky. I…uh, I am going to be…uh…seeing a lawyer about a house I'm selling. I was, um…planning to rent a place. For a week or so. Well…" Jake shrugged, glancing outside. "It's been a long day of driving."

"Where'd you come from?" asked the bartender.

"Louisville," Jake answered.

"You drove all the way up here in this weather?" the bartender asked, wide-eyed.

The patron at the bar reared back on his barstool. "That's a long way on a day like this."

"You can say that again," Jake said, already tired of the conversation.

No one said a word as Jake felt the men sizing him up. He was hoping he wasn't slurring his words, but he felt he might have been…or was about to. He focused on what he needed and asked, "Is…uh, is there a place, like a hotel or something around here?"

The bartender frowned. "Well, we are under renovation, and the Sandusky Hotel is completely closed up for repairs. They don't get business this time of year."

"Oh, you're kidding," Jake said, swallowing. He shook his head, trying to think. He was nearly out of gas, and he wanted nothing more than to sleep it off. Ten beers had kept him company on the long ride, and now he needed to lie down.

"As I said, our little inn is kind of under renovation, but we have a room upstairs that could hold you," the bartender said, surprising Jake, pulling him out of his thoughts.

Jake looked up, his eyes hopeful. "Oh, you have a room here? Um…can I rent it for the week?"

"Well, there are no frills, but it will give you a place to sleep."

Jake eyed the bar. It would be more than a place to sleep. He could get his drink here and probably work out a deal.

Jake said, "I've got $125 dollars. I need it for maybe a week?"

"You aim to be out of here before Christmas? It's a week from today."

"Oh, right. Christmas. Jeez, I…" Jake chuckled. "I almost forgot. Well, I probably need it until after Christmas."

The bartender thought for a moment, as if calculating, then said, "All right. $125, you say? That will be fine. We can take it one week at a time for now."

Jake fumbled in his pocket and pulled out his money. He had about $300, and he counted out $125 and handed it to the bartender.

The bartender extended his hand. "My name is Sal. This is Mr. Gill. He's going home now. I'll be closing up soon."

Jake asked, "Can I possibly get a sandwich and maybe a beer?"

"I got some ham in back. I'll fix you something quick. What kind of beer?"

"Draft is fine."

"All right. The first one's on the house, and the sandwich too, for tonight."

"Thanks," Jake said.

Sal turned his hat around, so the bill was facing backward. He went behind a curtain that led to a little storeroom and kitchen. He returned a few minutes later, smiling, and set down the ham sandwich, along with a jar of mustard and a knife. "Draft, you say?"

"Yes."

Mr. Gill stood up and drained his beer. "I'm going, Sal. See you next week. Have a merry Christmas. The Mrs. and I will try to stop in on Christmas Eve."

"You do that, Mr. Gill," Sal said. "Merry Christmas to you and the Mrs."

Sal set down the draft beer in front of Jake and swiped Mr. Gill's empty glass off the counter, all in the same motion. Then he turned his hat back around to face forward and said, "I'm afraid you'll have to finish that up in your room. I'll take you upstairs and show it to you. Then I have to go home."

"Do you live nearby?" Jake asked.

"Yes, I live a block away."

"Oh, okay," Jake responded, wondering why he had asked. Sal walked to the end of the bar, lifted the hinged part of it, went through, and came around to Jake's side. "Follow me, Jake."

Jake grabbed his sandwich plate and beer and followed Sal across the large wooden floor. The floor creaked all the way. They ascended the stairs on the other side of the large room opposite the old wooden bar area. The creaking of the stairs was almost eerie. The place gave him a brief shudder, like he'd felt as a kid going up to his room in the attic. But he knew a sandwich, a beer, and a place to sleep was all he could ask for on a night like this. It would do.

They reached the top of the steps and stepped through a door. Sal flipped a switch to turn on the hall light. "I wish I had a nickel for every time I flipped that switch," he said, chuckling. Jake half smiled, amused by Sal's mannerisms.

The hallway was thirty feet long and had faded maroon flowered wallpaper stretching the entire length. There were several doors, all closed, with numbers on them. The numbers were made of tarnished silver and looked like they had been there for a hundred years. Sal led Jake past number 1 on the right, then number 2 on the left, then number 3 on the right. When they reached number 4, halfway down the hall, they stopped. Sal opened the door. "This is the room. It looks out onto the street." He reached in and switched the light on, saying, "Well, I'll be a monkey's uncle."

"What is it?" Jake said, worried.

"Well, the bed's all freshened up, as if we'd been expecting ya. Someone must have done it recently. It's been a little while since we've had someone stay here."

"Oh, really?" Jake asked, feeling a bit confused.

Jake peered in, hesitant, and scanned the room. It was a large room with not much furniture. There was a plain wooden single bed against the far wall. A light blue comforter was turned down, with two pillows propped up against the headboard. Next to the bed was a nightstand in front of a window. A dressing chair stood next to it, just to the side of the window. In the corner, there was a small wooden dresser that looked to be seventy or eighty years old.

Sal watched Jake eye the room, then said, "It's not much, but it's cheap, and I think you'll find it's comfortable."

"Yes, um…it looks just fine. Thanks, Sal."

"Almost forgot," Sal said as he stepped into the hall. He took two steps down and opened a door with no number on it. "This is the bathroom. You can shower here. There are linens on the shelf in the closet."

"Great. That sounds good," Jake said.

"All right, Jake. I'll see you tomorrow." Sal turned his baseball hat around to face backward.

"What time do you open?" Jake asked as Sal was stepping away.

"11:00 tomorrow morning. I'll be there just before."

"Um…" Jake murmured, looking around. "What if I have to leave?"

"Yes, sorry. I almost forgot. There is a back door down those steps." Sal pointed to the other end of the hall. There was an identical staircase at the other end of the hall, leading downward. Sal said, "Here's the key. It leads to the back parking lot. You can come and go as you please. The door that leads to the bar will be locked when I go down. Is there anything else?"

"No, thank you. I'll see you tomorrow," Jake said, as he watched Sal go down the steps with a wave.

Jake went into his room, put his bag on the bed, and rummaged through it. He pulled out the formal letter he had received from the attorney only a few days earlier. It was this letter, along with his wife's, that had given him the idea to come to Sandusky. He took it out of the envelope and carefully unfolded it. It was his last hope.

December 10, 1970

Dear Mr. Butterfield,

I have made very little progress selling the old home and land owned by your grandfather. There seems to be little interest in the property due to its extensive disrepair. However, I want to propose buying it myself.

I was a close friend to your grandfather, and I would consider it a favor to him to offer you $13,000 for the property. I have little use for it, but, again, I feel I owe it to your grandfather to help you out.

If this seems satisfactory to you, call me and I will arrange the final papers, as well as the transfer deed. I will also make arrangements to wire the funds to you.

Sincerely,
Wayne Pearsall, Attorney

Jake started to drift off, then snapped his head up and opened his eyes. He was seeing double, and he was still holding the letter. He shook his head and said to himself, "No, Mr. Pearsall, I will need more money than that. Lots more than that."

Jake let the letter slide on the floor as he drifted away.

Monday

Frannie opened her emerald eyes and sighed. Another day was upon her. They all seemed to blend together lately, and she longed for a change. She lifted her head from the pillow and turned, looking out her upstairs window onto the back lot behind the Volstead. "Oh dear," she said. There was snow, and lots of it. Another year was passing. Fall had ended, and another season was in the books. When would it ever end?

She threw off her blanket and swung her tiny feet onto the rug that lay next to her bed. She could feel the draft upon her feet. She shivered and said to herself, "I hate the winter."

She got up and began her morning routine, washing herself, putting on fresh clothing, combing her long auburn hair, and picking out a modest dress to wear. Today it would be the blue flowered one, the one Big Rosie had given her as a gift long ago. There were other dresses, but this one was her favorite, partly because it had come from Big Rosie.

Rosie Volstead was the owner of the establishment. She was Frannie's boss. Whatever Rosie said or wanted was the law around the Volstead.

Frannie looked into the mirror as she pulled her hair over one shoulder and smoothed it. She paused for a moment, smiling at herself. But soon her sorrow returned, and her smile fell into a look of dismay. She wiped a tear, glancing up, wondering when the sorrow would ever leave.

For many years now, she had known it could not—no, it would not, for she had caused it. It was her fault, mostly, and she had accepted that. Lately, though, she could feel a new hope trying to break its way through, though, in truth, part of her was afraid to let it.

She glanced down at the top drawer of her dresser, the one that held the picture, the drawer she could not get herself to open. She gulped, knowing she should open it and believed she would, someday, when it was time. She reached her hand toward it and stopped. Today was not the day. Soon, though. Soon she would.

A knock at her door startled her out of thought. From the familiar sound, she already knew it was Big Rosie.

"Come in," Frannie said happily.

Rosie opened the door and gave Frannie the warm, tight-lipped smile she had given all the girls for ages. "How are ye today, Frannie?"

"I'm doing well, Rosie."

"There's a patron here today. You'll have to clean the place extra well."

"I will. What room?"

"He's in Room 4, right down the hall from ye."

"Okay, Rosie. I'll take care of it."

"He'll be going out around lunchtime, I suppose. So, take care of the bar area, the parlor, and speaking rooms first, then see to Room 4 straightway after lunch."

"All right, Rosie. What's for dinner tonight?"

"I am making us shepherd's pie."

"Oh, I can't wait. It was my favorite as a little girl. My granny used to make it for us."

"Aye, as did mine. Now enough about the shepherd's pie. Do a good job today, Frannie, and make me proud of ye."

"I will, Rosie. I will."

Rosie smiled warmly and closed the door.

Frannie smiled too, savoring the moment. She loved Rosie; she had for a very long time. Rosie had saved her, had become a mentor and practically a second mother to her. Rosie was that for most of the other girls too—at least, to the ones she liked or who didn't give her trouble. They all knew Rosie had their backs. But that was back in the old days, and the old days were no more.

~ ~ ~ ~

Frannie donned a yellow apron over her flowered dress. She picked up her duster and rags, then went down the old wooden steps, dusting the rail. She wiped the bar down carefully, then dusted all the stools and tables. Frannie backed out of the room and marveled at her work. The bar was cleaned to perfection. She sat for a moment, thinking about her grandmother.

Frannie had learned to clean from her grandmother, Peggy, who had helped raise her. Grandma Peggy lived next door to her growing up, so Frannie would see her nearly every day. She was like a second mother, or even like a first mother to her, as Frannie's real mother worked long hours as a seamstress.

Grandma Peggy also had emerald eyes and brown hair. She was of medium height and slim, with strong bones. She had a sweet Irish brogue that sounded like music to Frannie's ears. She was from the village of Tiernar in County Mayo in the barren west of Ireland. The people who came from that part of Ireland were hardworking, no-nonsense people. Grandma Peggy was all of that, but she had a kindness about her, and also, as she called it, "a wee bit of devilment." Oh, how Frannie loved her and missed her.

Almost daily, when Frannie was a child, Grandma Peggy would come over and fix her breakfast. Afterward, they would start at one end of the house and clean each and every room thoroughly, backing their way out, kicking or sweeping the pile of dirt into the hall. Then they'd close the door and go to the next room to repeat the ritual. Frannie always marveled that Grandma Peggy made cleaning feel effortless.

She had died twelve years earlier, when Frannie was only eleven, and Frannie missed her terribly, and thought of her every day. Frannie was not sure if this was out of habit or respect, but at an early age she'd adopted her own minor version of Grandma Peggy's Irish brogue.

Frannie finished her last duties well before the place opened at 11:00. Then she went into the kitchen, made herself a ham sandwich, and went up to her room to have lunch, as was her routine.

Big Rosie had her own routine. It was around this time every day when she went out to attend noon mass at St. Mary's on Central Avenue, about a ten-minute walk. Frannie had been invited, but she could not go. St. Mary's was where she had been married, and... well, she didn't deserve to obtain the comfort that going to church could bring. After all, it had been her fault, and there was no going back. It was too late.

But going to church every day helped Rosie. She always came back with a gleam of hope in her eye. Frannie got to bask in that glow, and she was grateful just the same as if she herself had gone.

~ ~ ~ ~

When Frannie finished eating, she peeked down the hallway toward Room 4. The door was closed. Frannie got her key and went down to clean it. She knocked, listened carefully, knocked again, then inserted the old wrought-iron key into the door and turned it, unclicking the lock.

She peeked in to be sure no one was still sleeping. Then, when sure the coast was clear, she stepped inside, leaving the door open, as was Rosie's rule.

Frannie frowned. There were two empty beer cans on the dresser and a half pint of whiskey next to the bed. The room was unkept, even after one day. There was clothing on the floor, the bed was unmade, and disheveled papers were on top of the table near the window. "Well, it looks like the cat's dragged in someone who is very messy."

She went to work, careful not to disturb anything that should not be disturbed. She made the bed, but it made her wince, as the very sheets smelled like alcohol. She realized the man must be a drunkard. She finished up and went to her room to read and relax for the rest of the day.

~ ~ ~ ~

Once in her room, Frannie fixed herself a cup of hot tea and sat by the window. She thought back to the old days, to some of the drunken men who had roamed these very halls years ago. They were rude and raucous, and they took no heed to treat any of the girls like ladies. It mattered not that they were women of the night. They were women, and they were there to take care of these men. It always unnerved Frannie that the patrons thought this was acceptable, that because they were men, they could get drunk, that they thought they were funny and the girls enjoyed it. She knew they did not at all, but they endured it because it was their job.

Rosie kept most of them in line. She never backed down from those men who got out of control—she'd punched a few in the noses when necessary, and a wallop from Rosie was like a wallop from the country sheriff. It was no small matter.

Rosie's wallops were followed by banishment, and this all the men feared, because they somehow needed this place.

It mattered not that most of them were married, or betrothed, or even passing through with no notion of who would entertain them. They convinced themselves that they deserved to frequent such an establishment.

But it didn't matter anymore. Rosie had suddenly brought an end to it all, and Frannie never knew why. One day, they were all here, carrying on with the business as usual. The next day, they were all gone, except for her and Rosie. Frannie did not mind in the least. She disliked being associated with the purpose of the place: that of entertaining men. Like the others, though, she'd had to endure them. Though she was only there to cook and clean, she still had to endure it all. Now that the place was just a bar and inn, Frannie felt more at home.

~ ~ ~ ~

Jake walked for about a half mile, asking people for directions until he found his way to the Port Sandusky Restaurant. It was a small place, cramped in many ways but with ample room once you sat down. He sat at the counter and ordered eggs, toast, bacon, and a glass of tomato juice to soothe his hangover.

When the waitress brought his food, he asked for and received a few aspirin.

When he finished eating, he took a dime out of his pocket and went over to the phone. He pulled the letter from his other pocket and dialed the number on it.

After several rings, a man answered. "This is Mr. Wayne Pearsall."

"Hi, Mr. Pearsall. This is Jake Butterfield."

"Jake Butterfield," Mr. Pearsall said, searching. "Oh, yes. Hi, Jake. How are you?"

"I'm good, I guess."

"Did you get my letter?" asked Mr. Pearsall.

"Yes, that is what I want to talk to you about."

"Okay, shoot," Mr. Pearsall said.

"Well, I am actually in town. I was hoping I could talk with you in person."

There was a long pause. Then Wayne cleared his throat and said, "In town? Here, in Sandusky?"

"Yep," said Jake.

"I see. Well, why don't you come over?" Mr. Pearsall said, "I am in the Hogerefe Building on Columbus Avenue. Where are you now, Mr. Butterfield?"

"I'm at the Port Sandusky Restaurant," Jake said.

"Oh, okay. You are right around the corner. Tell Don and Sherrie you are coming to see me. They'll give you directions."

~ ~ ~ ~

Ten minutes later, Jake walked up to an old brick two-story building with the words HOGEREFE BUILDING etched in stone at the top. He wondered who Hogerefe had been to have gotten his name on a building. He was long gone by now, that was for sure.

On the wall was a sign: WAYNE PEARSALL, ATTORNEY AT LAW. Underneath, there was an arrow pointing up a long flight of dark oak stairs.

Jake trudged up the stairs, his headache pounding with each thud and creak of the old wood. By the time he got to the top, he was out of breath. He did not have stairs at his house back in Louisville.

Since his arrival in Sandusky, he seemed to be going up and down stairs all day long—it only served to remind him of his wife's comments about his physical condition. He didn't disagree with her, but now that he was facing a new life—a life alone—he understood she was right. He was out of shape, big time.

He paused at the top of the stairs, then turned down a long hall that led to a dark oak door emblazed with gold lettering.

He knocked, and when no one answered, he cracked open the door and called out, "Hello?"

"Jake?" came a gruff voice from an interior room.

"Yes."

"Come in."

Jake stepped in, passing a secretary's desk that looked like it had not been used in a long time. Boxes were strewn all over and around it. They looked to be in some kind of order, just not the order in which a secretary would keep them in.

There was an open door that led to an office. A tall, thin man with wavy gray hair walked out smiling, with his hand extended. "Hi, Jake. I am Wayne Pearsall. Call me Wayne."

"Hi, Wayne. Thanks for seeing me."

"Please, come in," the lawyer said. He turned gracefully and walked into his office, motioning for Jake to follow.

Wayne looked to be somewhere near seventy years old, but the office looked older. It had dated maroon and green wallpaper and three large, wooden-paned windows that looked out onto the street. There were no blinds. The desk was large. A bookshelf was on the side wall—dark oak also—and packed with volumes of legal research books. The entire place had an old, antique feel to it, like the Volstead Speak Easy Bar.

Jake sat down in one of the two chairs in front of the desk as Wayne took a seat.

"So, you received my letter?" Wayne said.

"Yes, that is why I came. You see, I need a little more for the property than you offered."

Wayne frowned for a moment, but then reassumed his smile. "Well, Jake. I am not sure if you understood my letter completely, but I was making you an offer as a favor to your grandfather. He came to me almost thirty-five years ago. We did his will, and he did not want the property to go to your father, so he stated that it was to be held in a trust until he died, or you turned forty, whichever came first."

Jake shook his head and wondered aloud, "I knew none of this. What happened between them?"

"They had some kind of falling out. I was never told the reason."

Jake lowered his gaze. His whole life, his father had left him in the dark about a lot of things, and this, of course, was one of them.

Mr. Pearsall interrupted his thoughts. "When your father died last year, I contacted you and started the process of listing the house. The problem you have, Jake, is that the house stood empty for so long that it is no longer habitable. It really needs to be torn down. So, you can imagine why no one wants to buy it."

"I see," Jake said, fidgeting. He was thinking about his mounting IRS debt. He felt desperate, but he could not show it. He had come all the way here for this moment. He asked, "Would you be willing to take the price up to $20,000?"

Wayne reared back, and his frown reappeared. "That's a lot of money for that house. I was already offering you far more than it was worth."

"Well, I need more," Jake said excitedly, a feeling of fight or flight racing through his veins. "I have debts to pay."

Wayne sighed and glanced out the window. "Let me think about it. Where can I reach you?"

"I am at the Volstead."

"You're staying there?" Wayne said, surprised.

"Yes, they had a room available."

"What do you know," Wayne said. He stood and extended his hand, smiling again but not as warmly. "It was nice to meet you, Jake. I will be in touch soon. But I can't promise anything."

Jake started to turn, then stopped. "Was there anything left in the house?"

"Yes, there were a few old books and letters, things of that sort. Since Captain Butterfield was a hero at Gettysburg, I sent them to the library so they could add them to their collection. Your grandfather wanted that. They are being catalogued and evaluated right now."

"Can I see the papers?"

"Why, sure. I mean, of course. I will write you a letter you can take to the library."

"Is it nearby?"

"It's a five-minute walk from here."

Jake rose and thanked him, then left.

As Jake walked out, Wayne grimaced. "Shoot," he said. Had he made a mistake in telling Jake about the letters at the library. The last thing he needed was Jake falling in love with the nostalgia of the place.

Wayne turned to look out the window. His mind worked overtime, sorting out his options as well as his risk. He had not expected Jake to come to town. He had to act quickly.

~ ~ ~ ~

In the early evening, Jake sat at the Volstead bar, working on his third beer. He felt like having something stronger, but his budget would not allow it, not if he was going to last the week. An older man, balding slightly, walked in, shaking the snow from his boots and unwrapping his scarf.

"Hello, Sal."

The bartender looked up from washing a glass, smiled, and said, "Hello, Jim. How's the weather out there?"

"It's cold as you-know-what."

"I figured as much," Sal said. "What can I get you?"

"Give me a bourbon, straight up."

"You got it."

Jake watched the man curiously. He was dressed like some sort of professional, and a seasoned one at that. He wore a maroon scarf draped over an expensive, camel-colored wool trench coat. His hair was thin at best, and mostly gray with remnants of some strands of black. He walked over and turned to Jake, saying, "Hello there, stranger."

"Hi," Jake said, happy to meet a fellow traveler of the barstools of the world.

"Jim," the man said, extending his hand and adding, "Jim Ruthsatz."

"Jake, Jake Butterfield." Jake shook the older man's hand.

Jim considered Jake's name and asked, "Butterfield? That's a famous name around here. Any relation to Captain Butterfield?"

Jake replied, "Yes. Archibald Butterfield is my great-grandfather. He and Captain Butterfield were brothers."

Jim said, "Your great-grandfather? Wow, that goes back a long way. Are you new in town?"

"Well," Jake sighed, wishing he had not opened his mouth, "I am here to see a lawyer about selling the place. We are settling my grandfather's estate; he was Archibald's son. I am the only heir left."

"Oh, yes, I heard they were selling the place. Why didn't any of Captain Butterfield's children inherit it?"

Jake slowly shook his head. "There were no children, as far as I know. I think he had a wife, and maybe a son, but I think they died. The property transferred to my great-grandfather Archibald after the captain died."

Jim said, "You know, then, that Captain Butterfield was a hero at Gettysburg."

Jake nodded. "Yes, I've heard that over the years, but I never paid attention. We live pretty far away from here. I was actually surprised to get the letter from the lawyer."

"The 'only heir' you say. That's odd," Jim remarked.

Jake motioned for Sal to set him up another draft, then continued, "My own grandfather died several years back. He owned the property. I didn't know much about it. But recently, I lost both of my parents. Then I got the letter from the lawyer. It caught me by surprise, but here I am. I think, though, there was some kind of holdup." Jake didn't want to tell Jim and Sal that the lawyer couldn't sell the place because it was falling into disrepair. He was embarrassed.

Jim said, "Captain Butterfield was a great man."

Jake nodded with a half-smile, nervously took a long sip of his beer, then exhaled. "Unlike my predecessors, I've not made any marks in this world." He laughed and took another sip, wiping his mouth and turning to see his newfound acquaintance's reaction to his clever summation.

Sal chimed in. "Oh, you will make a mark in this world, Jake. Don't worry. All the Butterfields have made their mark in the world. And you will too." Sal paused, then turned his ball cap around; it was facing frontward now.

Jake tried to change the subject. "So, what do you do, Jim?"

"I'm an accountant."

"Oh," Jake said, swallowing. He shook his head. "Taxes are my downfall."

"Oh, you have tax troubles?"

"Yeah…about three years ago, I made about $20,000 on a book that sold really well. I invested most of it in a book-marketing program, so I didn't think I had to worry about taxes."

"Never reported the income?"

"No," Jake said, frowning. "Didn't think I had to, since I spent the money on book expenses."

"How much do you owe?" Jim asked.

"Last I heard, about $11,000."

Sal's eyes widened, "Well, I'll be a monkey's uncle. That's a lot of money in this day and age, Jake."

"You can say that again," Jake said, cringing.

"I can help you, Jake," Jim said. "Come and see me after Christmas. I know what to do."

"Really?" Jake said. He was beginning to like the people of Sandusky. They were peculiar, to be sure, but there was something about them.

Sal asked, "Jake, have you sold any more books?"

Jake lowered his gaze. "No, I ran out of ideas around the same time."

"So, let me guess," Jim said. "Your wife is upset about the taxes you owe."

"Yep," Jake said slowly, staring blankly at the bottles of liquor behind the bar. "She says I'm a drunk, and she's leaving me."

Sal's brow furrowed. "Sorry to hear that, Jake. You seem like a good man to me."

Jim nodded subtly, as if steadying himself, then asked plainly, "Are you…a drunk?"

Jake felt the blow, but he knew the man meant no harm. Jim was challenging him, the way any older man might challenge a younger man to be honest with himself.

Jake rubbed his chin, considering his answer, then said, "I have been drinking a lot the last few years, but I'm hoping this inheritance will help me get my life back on track."

Jim nodded, considering his reply, then said, "Money won't help you, Jake."

Sal turned toward Jim and chimed in, "Well, I'll be darned. I want to hear this one." Sal then turned his ball cap around, so it faced backward. He leaned against the bar with his arms crossed, waiting for Jim to continue.

Jim glanced over, waited for Sal to get settled, then said, "You need more than money to get your life back on track, Jake. You need a reason, or a purpose." He added, "I hope you don't mind me saying all that. I like you. I'd like to see you get through this."

"Well, I'll be darned," Sal said again. "That was good, Jim. That was really good."

Jim nodded with a proud smile on his face.

Jake watched the two men form conclusions about him, then said, "It's funny how people see right through me lately."

"Hey," Sal said, "don't worry about a thing, Jake. You're among good people here. This old place is not called a 'Speak Easy Bar' for nothing. We speak easy around here—nice and easy, nice and friendly."

"Thanks," Jake said, nodding at Sal.

Jake stared into his glass. Things had been hard. His marriage, his work, his writing. It had all been a disaster, and for a long time.

Jake started to take the last sip of his beer, but he stopped midway through and set the glass down. "Goodnight."

"Goodnight, Jake," Sal said.

Jim added, "Come see me after Christmas."

"I will," Jake said.

Tuesday

On Tuesday morning, Jake woke up late with a pounding headache. He was growing tired of his hangovers, and as usual, he vowed to let this be the day he stopped drinking for good—or at least stopped drinking so much.

He glanced at the clock. It was 10:45. He shook his head, slowly got up, and changed out of the clothes he had passed out in. He showered, put on a clean pair of jeans, a blue flannel shirt, fastened his thick brown belt, and put on his blue Converse shoes. He would be doing some walking today, so he had decided against his brown loafers.

He picked up a few papers from the desk, opened his bedroom door, and stepped into the hall. Just outside his door was a tall woman. Jake stepped back. "Oh! You scared me."

"I did, did I? Well, I'm sorry," the woman said with a broad smile, as if entertained by his reaction.

"No...it's okay," Jake said, "I didn't expect to see anyone."

Jake studied the tall woman standing before him. She looked ruddy and straight, with pinned-back brownish gray hair. She wore a full-length brown skirt and a tan blouse, with stockings and black-soled, thick-heeled shoes. There was a string of pearls around her strong neck. She looked sturdy, with piercing blue eyes and a tight-lipped smile on her face.

She reached out her hand. "I'm Big Rosie. I run this place."

Jake took her hand and felt her stern grip. "Oh, I didn't know. I'm Jake."

"Aye, Jake, where are ye from?"

"Louisville," he replied.

"Aye, I spent time there years ago. In my early days."

"Oh, is that right?" Jake found her thick Irish accent amusing.

"Well, is your room satisfactory?" she asked.

"Oh, it's just fine. Thanks for cleaning it yesterday."

"I'll thank Frannie for you. It's she who cleans it."

"Yes, well, it's nice to meet you, Rosie," he said, stepping away.

"It's nice to meet you too, Jake. I'll see you before long."

Jake nodded and walked to the end of the hall. Then he turned to ask her a question, but she was already gone.

~ ~ ~ ~

At 11:45, Jake walked out the back door of the Volstead on his way to the library. He'd purposely left the back way, not wishing to see Sal. He usually felt embarrassed when he was badly hungover, and today was no different. As his mother used to tell him, his moods were easily detectible, written all over his face, even more so when he was hungover. It was one of the reasons his wife had railed against him so often in the last few years. There was no hiding his drinking from her. Even when he did it in secret, she could see it on his face the next day.

Jake turned the corner and headed for the library. The brisk wind of the cold winter day shook him out of his thoughts. He walked several blocks, past the Port Sandusky Restaurant, and then past Mr. Pearsall's office. Five more minutes, and he would be at the library.

Perhaps this was the start of something. Perhaps he'd find out some interesting facts about his great-grandfather, Archibald. His father had told him nothing about his lineage. Jake lamented their broken relationship and could not understand why it had to be that way. And now his father was dead. There would be no fixing things.

Perhaps, though, he could do something to make his heritage proud. Perhaps he would find some interesting facts, and he could write a story. Maybe it could be about Archibald, maybe about Archibald's famous brother, Captain Butterfield. Maybe it could be fiction made of facts he learned about the old house's history. The writer inside him was getting excited. An old part of himself, one that had been dead for a very long time, was beginning to stir.

His plan was beginning to form. He would learn all he could over the next week and simultaneously work on getting Wayne to pay more for the house. Then, when the price was as high as he felt it could go, he would cut a deal and leave town.

The walk to the library was more difficult than Jake had imagined. It had started to snow, and the wind was piercing. Jake wondered if there would be any accumulation. He pulled his jacket collar up to shield the wind. The street was busy, with many people coming and going in all directions. Up ahead, his eyes were drawn to a big sign. In lit-up yellow letters, it said, OLD IRONSIDE BAR. He paused for a moment, and the voice in his head started.

Jake, you have time for a quick drink. Jake put his head down and started walking again, but then he stopped. The voice went on. *Jake, one small drink to warm your bones will be good for you.* He turned around, looking at the bar sign again as the voice continued. *One drink isn't going to kill you, Jake. Besides, you've earned it. You have a great plan to turn things around.*

Jake nodded to himself in assurance, as he agreed with his own line of thinking. He walked over to the bar, went inside, glanced around, and made his way to the nearest barstool.

"What'll you have?" a barmaid in her mid-thirties asked.

"Give me a draft beer. And set me up with a shot of whiskey."

"Coming right up."

~ ~ ~ ~

Mr. Bixby sat up quickly in his bed with a worried look on his face. He glanced out the window into the distance. There was trouble in the air. He could feel it. He stood up, barefoot, wearing only his long johns, and stretched. He wore them religiously from the first snowfall until St. Patrick's Day, which pretty much marked the end of winter. Mr. Bixby stood six feet three inches tall. He was unusually thin and had long, stringy black hair that barely touched his shoulders.

He went to the mirror and looked at his gaunt eyes and thin lips, bent at the corners in a slightly perceptible and permanent frown. He splashed water on his face, swirled some mouthwash around his mouth, and spit, then smiled.

He walked across the creaky oak floor of the third story in the old church, now abandoned and only containing some offices downstairs. It had once been a proud, vibrant Methodist church with an equally vibrant congregation. The upper floor gave him a modest place to stay and required little upkeep.

He reached the window and pulled back the curtain. From here, he could see most of the town. It was one of the highest points in Sandusky, and it was one of the reasons he stayed here. He liked being able to watch people.

His eyes swept the horizon, as well as the street below. He glanced to the north. The skies were dark, nearly purple, pregnant with snow. It was going to be another cold, snowy day in this wretched little town.

After dressing in his dark brown suit, he put on his boots, straightened his pale red tie, and went down the stairs. He had business to attend to.

~ ~ ~ ~

Three hours later, Jake felt someone tapping on his arm. "Sir, sir."

"Huh?" he asked, opening his eyes.

"You fell asleep, sir. I think it might be time for you to get on home."

"Home..." Jake looked around, disoriented, then remembered where he was. "Oh, yes. Do I owe you?"

"No, you already paid for your drinks."

"How many did I have?" Jake slurred.

"Four," said the barmaid, "of each."

Jake sighed and momentarily closed his eyes again, wishing he could sleep it off right there. He had a pounding headache, and, worse, he felt very low, knowing he had again succumbed to drink. He got up and stumbled out the door, making his way back to the Volstead.

~ ~ ~ ~

It was a gray, snowy, cold day. Jake's head continued to pound as he walked, enduring the winter winds from nearby Lake Erie that bit through his clothing. It took him a long time, but he finally made it back to the Volstead.

He walked into the old but now familiar establishment. Sal was standing at the bar, his cap turned backward. "Hello, Jake. Where've you been all day?"

Jake shook his head slowly and offered a half smile. "I have to get up to bed, Sal. I don't feel good."

"Well, can I bring you anything?"

"No, thank you."

Jake lumbered across the creaky wooden floor. He felt dizzy and paused at the bottom of the steps to balance himself. Then he went up slowly, holding tight to the rail, trying not to look as drunk as he felt. He made it to his room and opened the door. Before he could go inside, out of the corner of his eye, he saw Big Rosie come out of one of the rooms. He heard her heavy-soled shoes walking in his direction. He quickly went inside and closed the door, listening. He felt afraid, and he did not know why. Perhaps he was embarrassed. The footsteps paused outside his door, and Jake held his breath until they continued past.

Then he collapsed on his bed and passed out.

~ ~ ~ ~

Wayne Pearsall picked up his office phone and nervously dialed the home phone number of his business associate, Kathleen Williams. It rang several times, then went to voicemail. Wayne waited impatiently, then said, "Kathleen, this is Wayne. I need to talk to you about the property on Railroad Road. I want to be sure of something before I finalize some plans. We talked before. Please call me as soon as you can."

Wayne grimaced. Kathleen's cousin was on the board of the Cedar Land company. He and she had plotted to buy two adjacent properties, that they knew would be very valuable to the company. Jake's land was one of them.

He hung up and pulled out a map of the area and spread it out on his desk. The property on Railroad Road was circled, as was an adjacent property. That one was more carefully outlined in a different color, with a check mark on it, as he had purchased it just a year earlier. A larger property, just behind the two on Railroad Road, had markings on it that read, "Cedar Land Acquisition." Wayne smiled, nodded, then folded the map back up.

Just then, his phone rang. "Wayne Pearsall."

"Wayne, it's Kathleen."

"Hi, Kathleen. I needed to be sure that Cedar Land is still planning to move forward next fall. Any news?"

"Like I told you, Wayne. It's a done deal. They have to have the land to build the new hotel for the sports teams."

"All right. Is the price range still where we discussed?"

"If anything, it's going to go up. We will make more than we planned."

Wayne smiled. "That's what I needed to know."

~ ~ ~ ~

Hours later, Jake woke up and glanced at the time. It was 8:30 at night. He had been sleeping for over three hours, and his head was still pounding. He looked out the window. It was dark outside. The sound of Christmas music was playing softly over the loudspeaker of the hardware store across the street. Jake climbed out of bed and onto the chair that overlooked the street. It was snowing harder now. Several inches had accumulated. It reminded him of his first night in Sandusky. He was supposed to use this trip as a reset. But here he was, drunk again, with no purpose in life. He had no place to live either, he realized. He lowered his head in shame, thinking of his wife's hurtful words—words he deserved. He thought of Jim at the bar, asking, *Are you a drunk?*

Deep down, Jake knew he was not really a drunk. He was just lost, and depressed, and he didn't know what to do about any of it. He did not see any way through. He lowered his head.

"God, please help me. I want to change. I just don't know how." He closed his eyes and steepled his hands over his nose and mouth, breathing in slowly, feeling his breath warm his face.

A tiny yellow bird landed on the windowsill, startling him. It chirped and hopped a few times, making tracks in the fresh snow, then left. Jake wondered if it was an answer to his prayer, as birds of this type were not usually out in the winter. Was this some kind of sign? Maybe God had not abandoned him? He went to the bathroom, took a hot shower, then went back to bed.

Wednesday

Early on Wednesday morning, Frannie quietly knocked on Rosie's door.

"Come in, Frannie," Rosie said in her thick Irish accent.

Frannie opened the door, smiling. "I just wanted to say good morning to you, Rosie."

"Well, good morning to you, young lady. Sit down and I'll pour us a cup of tea."

Frannie walked in, glancing around Rosie's kitchenette. Rosie had the largest of all the rooms at the Volstead. And why should she not? She was the owner of the place.

Frannie sat down, admiring the old painting on the wall of Rosie's kitchen. It was a famous painting of a young French boy and girl, bowing their heads in the field to say the Angelus prayer. It was one of Frannie's favorites. Her Grandma Peggy used to stop every day at noon and recite the prayer with Frannie in her soft Irish accent. Frannie's memories drifted. She remembered it like it was yesterday.

Grandma Peggy would say, *The Angel of the Lord declared unto Mary.*

Frannie would reply, *And she conceived of the Holy Spirit.*

And they would say the Hail Mary together.

Then, Grandma would say, *Behold the handmaid of the Lord.*

Frannie would reply, *Be it done unto me according to Thy word.*

And they would say the Hail Mary together.

Finally, Grandma would say, *And the Word was made Flesh.*

Frannie would reply, *And dwelt among us.*

And they would say the final Hail Mary. They would then bless themselves and go about their day. Grandma told Frannie that pausing to remember Jesus and Mary gave them grace for the day, grace they needed in this world. It was a prayer Frannie cherished, not only because of her grandmother, but because of its simplicity, its brevity.

Rosie poured the tea, noticing Frannie admiring the picture. "You like that picture, Frannie."

"I do," Frannie confided. "It reminds me of when life was simpler, when young men and women relied on God for everything."

"Oh, I think those days are still with us, Frannie. I know they are for me. Now even more than when I first... Well, even more now."

Frannie wondered why Rosie paused, but she never questioned Rosie. Rosie's life was far more complicated than Frannie's simple life had ever been. Rosie had come from the south and somehow ended up owning an establishment the likes of the Volstead, which was no easy task for a woman.

Frannie sipped her tea, then said, "I will start downstairs again today and get up to the stranger's room near lunch."

"You may have to give it a good cleaning today, Frannie. He was quite inebriated when he came in last night," Rosie said.

"I wonder why he drinks so much." Frannie said softly sipping her tea again.

Rosie considered her question, then replied, "Frannie, some people have things happen to them, or problems in their life they just can't face. When they don't address them, they can get stuck."

Frannie nodded. She understood, but the words saddened her. Rosie never said anything without intention, and Frannie wondered if her statement was geared toward her.

The two women sipped their tea, not saying much. Rosie seemed distant, looking out the window at the gently falling snow. Frannie thought it odd that Rosie wasn't talking, as she always had something to say.

After a few minutes of quiet, Rosie said, "So, another Christmas is upon us."

"Yes," Frannie replied. "It's in four days."

"Aye," Rosie said nodding. "I hope it is special this year."

"I do too, Rosie."

Neither of them spoke any more, just sipped their tea. They had grown accustomed to their conversations ending in quiet contemplation.

Finally, Frannie stood. "Thank you for the tea, Rosie."

"You're welcome, Frannie. Do a good job today."

"I will."

~ ~ ~ ~

Frannie got started in the bar area, as was her custom, mopping, dusting, lifting all stools, careful to get done before the bar opened. She finished the parlor and then made her way upstairs.

She knocked on the door of Room 4, and there was no answer. She took her key, quietly unlocked the door, and peered inside. The bed was empty. She went in, keeping her head down and the door open, as was Big Rosie's policy. As she walked toward the dresser, her eyes landed on a stack of papers. She went to straighten them so she could dust, and then saw the writing on them. She gasped and stepped back, putting her hand over her mouth.

Her mind raced back to days in her past, days she no longer wanted to be reminded of, the days of her sorrow. She gulped, suddenly hearing a groan behind her. She wheeled around, wide-eyed.

On a chair in the darkened opposite corner of the room was the stranger. He was asleep. He groaned again, then yawned and opened his eyes.

Frannie froze.

Though he had just awakened, the stranger seemed to instantly have full possession of his faculties. He wasn't the typical drunk Frannie had expected. He said, "Oh, you must be Frannie."

"How do ye know my name?" Frannie asked cautiously.

"Big Rosie told me you are the one who cleans the room. I'm sorry, I must have overslept."

Frannie stood uneasy, her shoulders drooped. She glanced at the floor. She wanted to leave, but he was in the path to the door.

Frannie already knew the answer to what she was about to ask, but she asked anyway, to be sure. "What is it that your name is?"

"Jake, Jake Butterfield."

"Butterfield, ya say."

"Yes."

Frannie looked down again, not wanting her emotions to get the best of her. She put her hands behind her back, hoping he wouldn't notice their trembling. She glanced over at the unmade bed, anxious to get out, and said, "I'll come back later, when ye're finished in here."

"All right," Jake said. "Give me about an hour."

Frannie nodded, lowered her head, and glanced to the floor as she walked past him and down to her room. She closed the door, went to her bed, and began to cry.

~ ~ ~ ~

Rosie sat in the back row of St. Mary's Church, quietly collecting herself after Mass. The church was decorated beautifully, with Christmas decorations adorning most of the altar, a scene she looked forward to every year. On the side altar, a Nativity scene was set up, with the baby Jesus covered by a sheet. There would be no unveiling of him until the start of Christmas Eve Mass.

The daily noon Mass had just finished, and a handful of people quietly lumbered down the middle aisle, passing Rosie on their way out. A few nodded, and most smiled, but no one said much inside the church—that was the way at St. Mary's. As they passed, Rosie's thoughts began to drift.

She had come to St. Mary's not long after the fire. At first, she had been afraid to return to church. Her life up to that point had been less than exemplary, and the regrets that burdened her every day had made her feel unworthy. One day, though, she met the tall man dressed in black. He walked past the Volstead while Rosie was sweeping the front porch. He stopped to talk with her for a few minutes—just small talk, nothing more. But he came back the following week when she was out sweeping again. This time, they talked a little more, and he introduced himself as Father Tom, a priest assigned to help out the pastor at St. Mary's.

It took a few more coincidental porch meetings before he invited her to come to daily noon Mass. She agreed to go, and when she arrived, he personally came over to greet her. He even introduced her to Ginny, who he said was a good friend of the parish. From that day on, Rosie felt welcome at St. Mary's, and from that day on, she started to come every day at noon. She sighed, realizing how long ago that felt like now.

Since the first day, Father Tom always came over after Mass to say hello, and Ginny did too. They were about the only people who did, but all the others were friendly. Rosie would smile at the other church patrons, nodding when she arrived and when she left. Their silence did not bother her, as she had grown accustomed to keeping to herself. But Father Tom and Ginny were the reason she came every day. Ginny had been helping out at the church for as long as Rosie could remember, at least as long as Father Tom had been there. There had been several other priests who also helped out at St. Mary's over the years, but none were as friendly as Father Tom.

Today was no different. When Mass was over, Rosie stood in the back pew, nodding and smiling at the faithful who were quietly leaving. Ginny came over and greeted Rosie in her soft voice. "Hi, Rosie. How are you today?"

"I'm well, Ginny. How's yourself?"

"Oh, not too bad for someone in their eighties!" Ginny said.

Ginny was smaller in stature, with long, grayish-black hair that she always kept in two braids hanging over her shoulders. She wore gray-framed glasses and had walked with a cane for as long as Rosie could remember.

"Well, you look grand, Ginny. Have you been knitting lately?"

"I have, and I have a small kitchen towel to give you later."

"Another one! Well, thank you, Ginny," said Rosie. "The good Lord knows I can use it. But I must pay you in some way for your kindness. I have an old Irish book I may give ye."

"Well, you better not wait too long," Ginny said. "At my age, you never know how long I will be here."

Rosie smirked, amused, and asked, "Well, will ye be here next week?"

"I think so," Ginny said, in a very matter-of-fact tone.

"We'll plan on that then."

Ginny smiled and walked to the back of the church.

Just then, Father Tom saw Rosie. He smiled, set the things in his hands on the altar, and walked hastily down the center aisle to the back.

"Hi, Rosie. How are you doing today?" Father Tom asked in his gentle, kind voice.

"Hello, Father. I'm only doing so-so."

"Oh, why is that?"

"Well, it's Christmas again. You know I get sad around this time, and I don't know why."

"It's that way for a lot of people, Rosie."

"I know. It just feels, well, like I'm stuck."

"You can change that if you want." His gaze lingered, and a small, knowing, wise smile came across his face.

"I know, Father. But I won't leave her. I've told you that before."

He nodded. "Yes, you have. And I admire you. Keep following your heart. It has not steered you wrong yet. And remember, everything will work out as it should."

Rosie lowered her glance, feeling a tear well up. He often told her everything would work out, and always at a time when she needed to hear it. She wiped the tear away and said, "Ah, now off with you, Father, before you get me to start crying."

He smiled. "I'll see you soon, Rosie."

~ ~ ~ ~

Jake went back to the Port Sandusky Restaurant to get some much-needed food into his weakened body. The heavy drinking was taking a toll on him. His furnace did not burn as brightly as it used to. It was taking longer and longer to recover from his bouts of drinking.

After finishing lunch, he went to a pay phone and dialed.

"Hello, Wayne Pearsall."

"Hi, Wayne; it's Jake Butterfield."

"Oh, yes. Hi, Jake. What can I do for you?"

"Well, I was wondering if you've given my proposal any thought?"

There was silence for several moments. Jake heard Wayne clear his throat. He didn't know if that was a good sign or a bad sign. The pressure of waiting for an answer was causing his head to pound worse than it already was.

"Well, Jake," Wayne said, cautiously, "to be honest, I should not be doing this. But I will agree to your price—on one condition."

"What's that?"

"We have to finalize it by Monday."

"Monday? The day after Christmas?"

"Yes. I'm leaving the office today at 3:00 p.m. to see my sister for Christmas. You're lucky you caught me."

"Monday is fine," Jake said. "I can hang around here till after Christmas."

"Okay. Come to my office Monday morning at 11:00. We can sign the papers, and I'll have your check ready.

"$20,000, right?"

"Yes, $20,000."

Jake hung up the phone and raised his fist in the air.

He had done it.

~ ~ ~ ~

When Rosie returned from church, she went in the back door of the Volstead and up the back steps to her room. As she passed Frannie's room, she heard weeping. Her brow furrowed, and she stepped backward and knocked on Frannie's door.

"Who is it?" came the shaky voice from within.

"It's Rosie."

Rosie opened the door. Frannie was sitting on her bed, hunched over, with her knees drawn together. Her eyes were stained red with tears.

Rosie ran over, sat beside her, and put her arm around her. "What is it, Frannie?"

Frannie took a few deep breaths, then told her everything. Rosie pulled her close. "Now, now, Frannie. Try not to cry. Everything is going to work out. You'll see. Now please take the rest of the day off and get some reading in. Come down to my place early in the morning. I'll fix us some breakfast and a warm cup of tea."

Frannie raised her tear-stained face and said, "I'd like that very much, Rosie."

Rosie hugged her warmly, then got up and quietly exited.

~ ~ ~ ~

Outside the room, Rosie's facial muscles tightened, and her brow furrowed again.

She marched down the hall to Room 4 and knocked on the door. She knocked again, louder this time. Then she took the keys from her dress pocket and opened the door. Rosie scanned the room. There was no sign of him, but the place was a mess, and there were empty beer cans on the floor, along with a nearly empty liquor bottle on the dresser.

Rosie closed her eyes, trying to calm her welling anger. She would deal with him later. She closed the door and went to her room.

~ ~ ~ ~

Jake paid for his lunch and headed to the library, something he should have done yesterday. It was already 1:00 p.m. when he carefully trudged up the broad, snow-covered stairs of the elegant library building in downtown Sandusky.

He opened the wide doors and beheld a Christmas tree lit up in the lobby. It seemed like one the most beautiful trees he had ever seen. It reminded him of the Christmas tree he and his wife had when they were first married. He paused for a moment to admire it and to remember what was. It saddened him and he wished things were different.

He went up to the front counter, where an older woman in a plain green skirt and white blouse greeted him. "May I help you?"

"Yes, my name is Jake Butterfield. I have a letter from my attorney introducing me and permitting me to view the archives." Jake handed her the letter and watched her read. She seemed puzzled for a moment, so Jake added, "I wanted to look at the historical items from my great uncle, Captain Butterfield's house."

"Oh, yes. I see!" the librarian exclaimed. "Yes, that is all very exciting. They just brought everything in last week. I don't think they have even started to unpack it yet."

"Is that so?" Jake remarked, even more interested now.

"Well, let me go ask the head librarian, Mrs. Kuns."

"Thank you," Jake said as he watched her enter a back room.

Jake glanced around the old library. There were rows upon rows of wooden bookshelves. The maroon carpet looked old, but it was clean and well cared for.

The woman returned. "Okay, I will take you to the room over there." She pointed to a large reading room. "There are a few boxes of things we are still working on. Mrs. Kuns says that because you have the letter from Mr. Pearsall, she is okay with you looking through everything. After all, you are the heir to these documents."

"Thank you," Jake replied.

The woman led him to the adjoining room, entered an ancillary room, and returned with a box. Then she went back and returned with another box, then another. "We have not started to catalog anything yet, so you can look as you like."

Jake thanked her, took off his coat, and hung it on the chair. Then he lifted the lid off one of the boxes. He felt a thrill he had not felt in a very long time. A pile of old letters and old newspaper clippings were inside. There were also some medals and uniform patches. He realized that with so much history contained in these boxes, part of him, perhaps the writer in him, was coming back to life.

He lifted the lid off another box. There was a neatly folded military uniform inside. Jake felt a shiver run up his spine, and he did not know why. Something about the uniform reminded him of the Volstead and this mysterious old town.

He opened the last box. Inside were several books, a few with papers and letters sticking out of the pages. He returned to the first box, being careful, as he pulled out a letter and sat back.

It was a letter from Jake's great-grandfather, Archibald, to his brother Captain Butterfield, before the Civil War started, before he had become a soldier.

Dear Bradley,

As you know, the coming war is one in which we must defend the cause of our glorious Union. I am enlisting next week in downtown Louisville. I do not know when they will ship me out. I imagine it will be after basic training. My hope is to bring those rebels into submission and end the war swiftly.

Will you take up the cause of freedom?

Your brother,
Archibald Butterfield.

Wow, Jake thought. This was all news to him. He never knew his great-grandfather Archibald had fought in the Civil War. Perhaps he did not shine like Captain Butterfield had, so no one talked about him. Perhaps that was why his life was of no consequence to his family. Jake's father never told him much of anything, and maybe that was one of those many things he had decided to leave out. Still, it was important. It should have been talked about. It should have been remembered.

He took out the next letter. It was from Captain Butterfield's wife, who wrote to him after he earned his captain's rank.

To: Captain Bradley Butterfield

My Dear Husband,

We rejoice at the birth of our son. He is a rugged little boy and so reminds me of you. It was a long labor, and the midwife helped me through the long night. But by morning I heard the voice of our little boy for the first time.

He is so beautiful. I long for the day of your return, so we can be a family. I plan to plant a small garden as soon as the weather breaks.

I miss you more than words can say. I long to hold you in my arms again and feel your warm lips upon mine. I love you, my husband.

Please take care of yourself. Let me know when you will be home.

Yours always,
Mrs. Marie Francis Butterfield

He picked up the next letter, which had been clipped to the previous one. It was a response from the captain to his wife.

My Dearest Darling,

I am so happy we have a son. I cannot wait to hold him and teach him everything he needs to know in this world.

I miss you too. The war is long and hard, but I am keeping myself safe.

There is rumor that a spring campaign will start soon. All furloughs are canceled for the foreseeable future.

As soon as I can, I will come home. I cannot wait to hold our little boy. What did you name him?

Don't forget I put my gold watch and some coins under the floorboard in the closet. If you need money, sell them. This war has taught me that nothing is of ultimate importance.

I long to kiss you and hold you, and that day will be here before we know it.

Sincerely,
Bradley

Jake reread the line about the gold watch and coins. *I wonder if they're still in the house....* He decided he should go and have a look around.

Holding the letter in his hand and reading the loving words the couple exchanged caused him to think about his wife. A sadness came over him. What had happened? They'd loved each other once. Perhaps they could again. If she would only let him be himself.

~ ~ ~ ~

At 1:30 in the afternoon, Mr. Bixby strolled down Market Street toward the Port Sandusky Restaurant. It was not his favorite place, but Tira, his best informer, would be there at the corner table near the door. He needed information.

He walked into a nearly empty place. The lunch rush was over, but there was Tira, sitting in the corner as he'd expected.

"Tira, how are you today?"

"I am doing well, Mr. Bixby. Sit down, please."

Mr. Bixby slid his long frame into the seat, stretching his legs toward the aisle to allow them room. "Tira, is there anyone new in town? Anything unusual happening?"

"You're really perceptive, boss. Yes, there's some writer guy staying at the Volstead."

Mr. Bixby's smile fell. "The Volstead?"

"Yep. He showed up a few days ago, best I can tell."

"What is he doing here?" Bixby asked.

"I am not sure yet. But he went to see that lawyer, Wayne Pearsall, just yesterday. It looked like he was headed to the library after, but instead he came into the bar. He's got a real problem."

"How do you know?"

"I can tell these things."

"Like what things?"

"Well, for one, he carries a notebook with him everywhere he goes. As I said, he was drinking, trying to write some things down on a legal pad. But he just kept scratching it out and crumbling the pages. I must have thrown away seven of them. He ended up getting smashed before he staggered back to the Volstead."

"An alcoholic?"

"Seems like it."

"Have you seen him today?" asked Bixby, concerned.

"Yes, just a little while ago. He walked by on his way to the library."

Mr. Bixby's brow furrowed. He glanced over his shoulder in the direction of the library.

Tira got up. "I have to go."

"Where are you going?" Bixby asked.

She winked. "To work."

~ ~ ~ ~

Jake noticed a tall, strange-looking man walk through the room. He seemed oblivious to Jake, which Jake found strange. He had expected the man to say hello, or nod, in that they were the only two people in the room. But instead, he came in, perused a far wall shelf, lingered for a few moments, then left.

Jake sighed and looked at his watch. It was only 2:30 p.m. He could do no more today, though. His mind felt exhausted. Too much was coming at him. He needed to stop for the day. He felt sick to his stomach, and his head still pounded. There was only one thing that would stop it: another drink.

He looked again at the clock, and his eyes widened. He remembered that he needed to catch Wayne. He went to the lobby, asked the librarian if he could use the phone, and anxiously dialed Wayne's number.

The phone rang seven times. Jake was about to hang up when finally Wayne answered.

"Hello?"

"Wayne, this is Jake Butterfield. Can I go see the house?"

"Oh, I don't know about that, Jake. It's really not safe to go in there. There is all kinds of damage and unsafe floors."

Jake frowned. "Well, I would probably still like to take a look. I can just stay outside, mostly."

"Well, I can't caution against it enough. But if you are certain, I'll need to give you the key."

"Okay," Jake replied. "Listen, I can come by right now. I am only five minutes away."

There was a pause, and Jake started to worry there would not be time. But then Wayne said, "Sure. Come right now."

" Oh, wait." Jake pulled a pen from his pocket and reached for something to write on. "What's the address?"

"Oh, I know this one by heart," Wayne replied. "It's 2500 Old Railroad Road."

"Got it," Jake said. "Thanks again, Wayne. I'll be right over."

Jake hustled back to the room. The tall man put on his hat and exited. Jake went in, glanced at the letters lying on the table, and wondered if someone had been looking at them.

~ ~ ~ ~

Jake left Wayne's office with the key in his pocket. In the near distance, he could see the bar he had gone to yesterday. He knew from experience that the only way to really stop his pounding headache was to have a drink. So, he walked over and went inside.

"Oh, welcome back," the barmaid said with a friendly smile.

Jake smiled back. He could already feel his spirits lifting. He had found a treasure trove of information, gotten his price for the house, and now he was going to look for gold in the floorboards. He was pumped. Jake rubbed his hands together and asked enthusiastically, "How are you doing on this lovely day, young lady?"

"Oh, I am fine," the barmaid said.

"I did not catch your name yesterday," Jake said.

"Tira," the barmaid replied with a warm smile.

"Nice to meet you, Tira. Set me up with a shot and a beer. Same as yesterday."

"First one's on the house today," Tira said.

Jake nodded and scooted onto the barstool. "Well, thank you. That sounds good to me."

~ ~ ~ ~

The darkness of a long winter evening had already descended on the streets of Sandusky as Jake staggered back to the Volstead. Most of the lights he saw resembled fuzz, as his vision was blurred. He reached the Volstead. From the street he could see Sal talking with a lone patron. Jake looked at his watch. It was only 6:00 p.m. He had time for one more drink, and he could not wait to tell Sal the good news. Maybe, finally, someone in this town would realize he was not a failure.

He opened the old wooden door and felt a rush of warm air on his face. It felt stifling for a moment, and his stomach churned.

"Hello there, Jake," Sal said enthusiastically. "Long time."

"Hi, Sal!" Jake boomed. "I come back triumphant!"

"Oh, really?"

"Yes. Pour me a beer Sal and fix me one of your famous hams."

"You mean a ham sandwich?"

"That's exactly what I mean!"

Sal said, "Coming right up, Jake."

Jake took a seat. He was breathing heavily. The snowy, cold walk from the library had taken more out of him than he realized. He was waking up, though. The wooziness he felt from all his drinking was starting to subside.

Sal set the beer and sandwich down. "So, what happened that you are so happy about, Jake?"

"I sold my house, Sal. The attorney is going to buy it from me."

"Well, I'll be a monkey's uncle. Who could have guessed that?"

"Yeah, he was a friend of my grandfather, and he is doing me a favor. He says he owes my grandfather one, and this is his way of paying him back."

"Congratulations, Jake! ! Will you be leaving us, then?"

"Not till after Christmas. First, I am going out to the old house to have a look around."

"Wow, fascinating. There is a lot of history out there, you know, with the captain and all."

"And my great-grandfather, Archibald. He was in the war too. I just found out today."

"Well, I'll be a—" Sal stopped, realizing he had just said he was a monkey's uncle. "Amazing, Jake. So great for you. Do you see any angles for writing in all this?"

"I really do. I am already on it. Trust me."

Jake knew he was lying. He had not even put one word to paper yet, and there were no ideas swirling around in his head either. He'd been lying more and more the last few years. He needed to stop, he knew, but it was difficult.

Jake finished his sandwich, drank his beer, and went up to his room. By the time he reached his bed, he was out for the night.

Thursday

The next morning, Frannie lay awake, deep in thought. Before the tragedy, before the great misunderstanding, her life had been so very beautiful, and it was supposed to always be beautiful. It was her happily ever after. They were young, and in love, and free to begin a new life, their life. But it turned into a nightmare, and she blamed herself. It was the reason for her sorrow, the reason for her private tears.

Frannie was the only child of an elderly couple in Detroit. She was quiet, unassuming, and kept to herself. When she entered a room, she always kept her gaze down—an effort to remain unnoticed. Despite her shy demeanor, one summer she met her husband at a dance in Detroit. She had just turned nineteen. The moment she saw him, she was in love. It seemed he was too. They danced all night. From there, a whirlwind romance ensued, and twenty-seven days after they met, he proposed.

They were married in Detroit. Shortly after, Frannie left her parents behind and moved with her husband to Sandusky, Ohio. Their life together was wonderful and unifying. For over a year, they worked together to fix up their home, and they enjoyed a quiet life together.

Then the war came, and Frannie's husband was drafted. Soon after he left, she realized she was pregnant. She sent word to him, but he was not able to come home. In Sandusky, she had no family, and their home was on the outskirts of the city, in the countryside. The days were lonely and hard. As her due date neared, she wrote again to her husband, but she had no way of knowing if he received her letters. When her labor pains started, a midwife came. It was a long, difficult night, but by morning Frannie had given birth to a son. A neighbor woman stayed on for a few days until Frannie was strong enough to take care of the baby.

Were it not for the monthly checks she received from the government, they would have starved. But Frannie fell in love with her little one, and her lonely life of waiting for her husband to come home suddenly changed to a life of caring for her child. She hardly had time to miss her husband.

There was a knock at her door. It was Big Rosie.

"Good morning, Frannie. I want you to start late today. Get some reading in and start at 10:00."

"That would be fine, Rosie. Thank you."

Rosie smiled, then turned and went down the hall. She looked back to make sure Frannie had closed her door—she had. Then Rosie knocked on the door of Room 4.

"Who is it?" came the voice from inside.

"It's Big Rosie. Open up, please," she said in a commanding tone.

Jake looked over at the door with surprise. He had not expected anyone, nor did he feel at ease about the voice's tone. He got up from the chair and walked across the room. The knock came again. "Just a minute," Jake said.

He opened the door. Big Rosie stood with her lips pressed tightly together and one brow furrowed.

"What can I do for you, Rosie?" he uttered nervously.

Rosie ignored the question, walked in, and said, "Close the door."

Jake did as she asked. Then he turned to face Big Rosie, who stood in the middle of his room with her fists on her hips, glaring at him.

She began. "Who are you to come in here, drinking every day and night and lying around until all hours of the morning?"

"I'm…uh…I'm sorry," Jake stuttered, his voice trembling.

"And I hear your name is Butterfield."

Jake swallowed. "I…I am. Is that a problem?"

"Why I oughta give you a good wallop on the nose, Jake Butterfield. I knew the Butterfields. They were not men who slacked off and spent their days and nights drinking." She raised her fist. "I'm telling you now: shape up, or else you'll be hearin' from me."

Her words and her glare carried the weight of a cannonball fired at close range. Jake swallowed. He thought of his wife's criticisms, which hurt just as much, but this was different. This didn't just offend or demean him. Rather, it pierced him to his core.

"Do we have an understanding?" Big Rosie said, clenching her lips as she straightened and released her fists from her hips. Something about her voice felt ancient, harsh, and yet profound.

"We do," Jake said, his knees beginning to tremble.

She scanned the room with fierce determination and asked, "Is there any drink in this room?"

"Yes, there is," Jake said sheepishly.

"Give it to me."

Jake swallowed again, then went into the dresser drawer and pulled out a half-empty bottle of whiskey. He then reached under his bed and pulled out a partial six-pack of beer. He handed them both to Rosie.

She looked at them, then up at him. "That's it, Jake. No more. Got it?"

"Yes, I got it."

She nodded, turned, and left.

Jake stood there stunned. He had never felt so intimidated as he had in those few minutes. He sat on his bed, bewildered, humiliated—and rightly so. No one had ever spoken to him with such force, and in an odd way it did not offend him, but rather it seemed to touch his very soul.

He looked out the window at the falling snow. Strangely, for the first time in ages, he felt free.

He glanced at the clock. It was 11:30.

~ ~ ~ ~

Rosie returned to her room. She never enjoyed having to chastise someone, but she knew that people often needed such a scolding, to help them redirect their course. She had given plenty of those talks to her patrons, and, indeed, to some of her girls throughout the years. Most were better off for it, though not all. Then she thought of Frannie and smiled. She had never had to offer a cross word to Frannie. Frannie was always so sweet, good, and kind that Rosie had never even thought to correct her. She loved this about Frannie.

She sat by the Christmas tree, thinking about the day so far and how much there was still to do. A sound caught her attention—a light tapping. She looked around. Was there a mouse running around? The sound was coming from the window. Rosie got up and went over. A pigeon, like the messenger pigeons of long ago, was sitting on the windowsill. A small white paper was attached to its leg. Rosie opened the window, untied the message, and then unfolded it.

It was a scrap of paper, hardly bigger than a chewing gum wrapper. Tucked inside was a small blue ribbon. Rosie stumbled backward. It was the ribbon she had given to Olga, one of her girls, long ago. It was the ribbon she had given to Olga before the fire. For some reason, she never saw Olga after that. Rosie often wondered if Olga had anything to do with the fire. Behind the ribbon, on the back of the small paper, written faintly in pencil, was H E L P.

"Olga, oh my. How… But where…"

Rosie closed the window, then opened it again. She quickly got another piece of paper and scribbled, "Where?" Then she affixed it to the pigeon's foot and shooed it away, whispering a prayer as she did. If one of her girls was in trouble, she was going to help. But it had been so long…. None of it made any sense.

~ ~ ~ ~

Jake hustled over to the Port Sandusky Restaurant, where he grabbed a hamburger and fries. Then he walked quickly to the library, careful to take the route that didn't pass by the bar.

Inside, he felt a surge of energy he had not felt in a very long time. He asked the librarian if he could continue with the two boxes. She went into a back room, then returned.

"I am sorry, Mr. Butterfield. Someone must have moved the boxes. I'll have a look around. Will you take a seat?"

"Sure," Jake said, surprised.

Jake waited. It was dead silent. He thought about all the good fortune that was coming to him. So much information about his past. Maybe, just maybe, he could turn things around. The very thought of that surprised him, because though he had wished for this many times in the past, for the first time in a long time, he felt it was realistic.

The librarian returned. "I'm sorry, Mr. Butterfield. This is highly unusual. Let me check one more place."

"No problem," Jake said, getting a little worried now.

As soon as the librarian left, an older lady with long black-and-gray hair tied back in two braids walked in carrying two boxes. Jake had never seen her before. She smiled at Jake and said, "Found them!"

"Oh, great," Jake said. He got up to thank the woman, but she disappeared back around the corner before he even made it to the counter.

The librarian returned from downstairs. "Well, I don't know what—" She stopped, seeing Jake with his hands atop both boxes. "Oh, where did those come from?"

"A lady just brought them over."

The librarian looked surprised. "A lady?" She turned looking behind her, confused, then said, "Oh, well. Okay, then. You can take them into the room you were in yesterday, Mr. Butterfield. Over there."

"Thank you," Jake said.

Jake went into the room the dimly lit room with a single large window, opened the box, and took another letter. This one was dated July 10th. It was on official stationery from the War Department of the United States.

To Marie Francis Butterfield

Dear Mrs. Butterfield

We regret to inform you that your husband, Captain Bradley Butterfield, is missing and presumed dead.

Your husband and his unit fought bravely in defense of a key position in the Battle of Gettysburg. His service to our nation will never be forgotten.

If we obtain more information, we will write to you immediately.

Sincerely,
General George Hunnicutt

Jake sat back in the wooden library chair and exclaimed aloud, "So that's how he died! I never knew." He was suddenly feeling emotional, thinking about the poor wife of Captain Butterfield, thinking about how hard life was back then and how easy he had it. More than anything, though, he felt the effects of Big Rosie's admonition. He had truly wasted his life for many, many years, and it saddened him greatly.

Out of the corner of his eye, he noticed someone walking toward him. He looked up. It was a man in black pants, a black shirt, and black shoes. It took a moment, but Jake realized he was dressed like a priest.

"Hello, sir," the man said, extending his hand. "My name is Father Tom."

"Hi, Father," Jake said, instinctively standing to shake the man's hand. "My name is Jake."

"Well, nice to meet you, Jake. Doing some research, I see?"

Jake scanned the papers in front of him, nodding. "Yes, looking into my family history."

"Very well. And what family are you from?"

"Butterfield. Captain Bradley Butterfield was my great-uncle."

"Oh, why sure. I know about him. The whole town knows that name. Actually, the library just received some historical documents."

"How do you know that?" Jake asked, surprised.

"I am one of the trustees. Our church is right next door." The man pointed in the direction of the church.

"Oh, yes. I've seen it. So, you are a trustee here?" Jake asked, confused. He didn't understand the connection between the church and the library.

"Yes, I volunteer. Since I'm always at the church, it's easy for me to help them out sometimes opening and closing."

Jake stood and shook Father Tom's hand again. "Well, it was nice to meet you, Father."

"Likewise, Jake," Father Tom said, as he smiled and left the room.

Just then, the librarian came in. "Mr. Butterfield, we will be closing soon."

Jake watched her head back to the desk. He looked at the boxes. There was plenty more to look through, but he decided a break would be good for him. He went over to the Port Sandusky Restaurant and got another hamburger before the dinner rush.

~ ~ ~ ~

Bixby sat at the bar, thinking, slowly and methodically stirring the drink Tira had made him. He needed to put a stop to all of this. But how? Long ago, he had masterfully set everything in motion, and now, somehow, it all felt fragile. These seemingly harmless events were all connected. He could feel it.

Tira approached and told Mr. Bixby what she thought he might want to know. "I didn't see him today."

"He's at the library," said Bixby.

"Is that a problem?" Tira asked.

"It could be. We shall see. I took the liberty of misplacing a couple of boxes, so it may be fine. I doubt anyone will find them."

Tira smiled widely. "You are a genius, Mr. Bixby."

"Don't patronize me, Tira. You should have seen all this coming."

Tira hung her head and turned to walk to the other end of the bar.

Mr. Bixby resumed his trance of thinking deeply and stirring his drink. Then he stopped and smiled. He had an idea. He picked up his drink, drank it quickly, and left.

~ ~ ~ ~

Rosie sat alone in her room, thinking. They had not had a guest in a while, and the fact that a Butterfield had arrived intrigued her. So many memories were coming back, memories she had somehow lost track of. Somehow, the years had hidden them.

There was a loud rap on her door. She turned, her brow furrowed, and stood quickly. Sensing trouble, she picked up her long stick and walked to the door. "Who is it?" she asked.

"It is Mr. Bixby, Rosie."

Rosie felt a shiver go through her. She had not heard that name in ages, and the last time she did, there was trouble—trouble she'd faced and dealt with, but trouble, nonetheless. He was not a good man.

She opened the door. "What do you want, Mr. Bixby. You have no business here."

"Oh, but I think I do, Rosie. I have complaints from some of the town's citizens. You are housing a boarder here, and this place is under renovation. It is illegal to have anyone here right now, is it not?"

Rosie glared. "Listen here, Mr. Bixby. I am going to give you exactly two minutes to get off this property." She raised her stick. "Or I'll give you a thrashin' worse than I did the last time you tried to bother me."

Bixby railed, "I'll bring the sheriff back with me, and we shall see who prevails, Rosie."

"Do your worst, Mr. Bixby, if you can. Mr. Butterfield is a guest of mine. He is no boarder."

"We'll see about that."

"Off with you, now. I'm warning you. Leave or else," she said, raising her stick higher than before.

Mr. Bixby gritted his teeth, turned, and stormed off.

~ ~ ~ ~

Frannie sat alone in her room, listening to the Christmas music playing across the street. There was a gentle knock at the door, and she jumped up and turned. "Who is it?"

"It's Rosie. Come down for tea."

"Oh, that sounds nice, Rosie. I'll be down in a few minutes."

~ ~ ~ ~

Rosie returned to her room and waited. She sat in one of the two chairs before the Christmas tree. The teacups were on the small table between the chairs. As they usually did this time of year, she and Frannie would enjoy the tree, have some tea, and talk about whatever Frannie needed to get off of her chest. It was something Rosie never tired of.

While Rosie waited, she thought of the first time she met—or rather found—Frannie. The Volstead was in full swing, bringing in lots of money for Rosie. One night, she heard a noise outside and found Frannie in the alley, rummaging for food. The poor girl looked near starving. As soon as she saw Frannie, with her disheveled hair and ragged dress, she knew it was her duty to help her, even if only because of her own past, to pay a good deed forward. Many years earlier, when Rosie was a teenager, she had been homeless on the streets of Louisville. If not for the help of a kind soul, she would have died.

Rosie had brought Frannie inside, let her take a warm bath, gave her a hot meal, and insisted she sleep in the bed in the basement, away from the other girls, who resided upstairs.

In the morning, Frannie had told Rosie the story of her baby's death. Rosie asked her if she had a home, and Frannie explained that a storm had caused a tree to fall on it, rendering it uninhabitable.

Then Rosie presented her with a life-altering deal: Frannie could cook and clean for her and the other girls who lived there. For that, Rosie would give her food and a small bed in the basement. Although Frannie seemed to be stuck in a bad situation, Rosie was going to see her through. She would not abandon the girl, nor leave her behind. It was just not her way.

Rosie never regretted the night she rescued Frannie from the streets. From the beginning, they had a connection Rosie could not explain. Over the years, Frannie had become like a daughter to her.

Rosie's thoughts were interrupted by Frannie's knock at the door. "Come, Frannie," Rosie said.

Frannie came in and asked, "Who was that you were arguing with earlier, Rosie?"

Rosie closed her eyes for a moment, unsure if she should upset Frannie. But she knew it was not right to hide it from her. "It was Mr. Bixby."

"Mr. Bixby. Why...I haven't heard that name in so long. What did he want?"

"He was trying to cause trouble. That's his way. I sent him packing."

"Well, I'm glad for that. Do you think he will leave us alone?"

"I think so, Frannie. Don't worry about a thing. Now, let's enjoy our tea."

~ ~ ~ ~

When Jake arrived back at the Volstead, the snow was heavy. Inside, he could see Sal leaning against the bar, looking at the TV. There was no one there. Jake walked in sheepishly, not wanting to engage Sal.

"Hello, Jake. Where've you been all day?" came the warm, familiar welcome.

"Well, I got a late start, but then I went to the library."

"Sit, sit down. Sit down. Tell me all about it."

Jake sat tepidly, realizing he'd come dangerously close to drinking again. He didn't want Big Rosie to think he wasn't sticking to his promise.

"What'll you have, Jake?"

"Actually, Sal. I'll have a coffee."

"Coffee, aye? Nothing to drink?"

"I'm going to try to lay off for a while."

"Well, I'll be a monkey's uncle," Sal said enthusiastically. He added, "That's good, Jake. That's good." He poured Jake a coffee. "Can I get you a sandwich?"

"You know, Sal, that would be great. Thank you."

Sal went into the back room and returned a few minutes later with a ham sandwich.

"So, what did you find out at the library, Jake?"

"Well, it looks like Captain Butterfield died at Gettysburg."

"Oh, really? I never really knew how he died," Sal said, adding, "but I think he is buried at the old home out on Railroad Way."

"Well, I'll find out," Jake said, nodding. "I'm headed over there tomorrow."

"That sounds good, Jake, and real interesting."

"Hey," Jake said, "I'm going to take this up to my room. How much do I owe you?"

Sal flipped his hat back around, saying, "Two bucks is fine, Jake."

"Thanks, Sal. See you later."

Friday

Frannie's sleep was restless. Too much was on her mind. When morning came, she stayed in bed, looking out the upstairs back window of the Volstead. She could hear the Christmas music coming down the alley from the hardware store across the street. It was the same alley that had brought her to the Volstead so long ago.

She was grateful Rosie had let her move to one of the upstairs rooms. They used to be reserved for the other girls, the ones who helped pay all the bills. But once they all left, Rosie invited Frannie to move upstairs, and she gave Frannie her own room.

Frannie remembered the day she met Rosie. She had run out of money weeks before and was starving. One night, she got the idea to look for food in the garbage cans outside restaurants. After midnight, she left her cold, barren house and walked over a mile into town. She felt weak and had to slow her pace.

When she got into town, all was quiet except for the noise and lights coming from the Volstead. She went down the back alley and over to the garbage cans. She stayed in the shadows, getting a glimpse into the windows along the way. Men and women were drinking in what looked to be a parlor. Some of the upstairs windows were lit up, others were dark, others were dimly lit, and in one, she could see a couple kissing.

She reached the back door of the Volstead. Not far away was a tin garbage can with a lid. She walked over quietly, carefully watching for anyone. As soon as she lifted the lid, she heard a voice and ducked back into the alley. A shadow with a raucous laugh lifted the lid, dropped something in, then slammed the lid back down and disappeared.

Frannie swallowed. She could smell food, and she was starving. She went back over to the can and lifted it. There, on a plate, were scraps of beef. She picked one up and thrusted it into her mouth, savoring every moment, her eyes watering with gratitude. She swallowed, then grabbed more, wrapping them in a towel she'd brought. It was not much, but it was enough to sate her hunger tonight and perhaps tomorrow morning too.

She headed home feeling a sense of hope she had not felt in a long time. She walked off the road and onto a dirt path that led up to her house. She went inside, lit the lamp, and sat on the cold chair by the unlit fireplace, slowly eating the leftover beef scraps, savoring every morsel. Finally, she fell asleep in her chair.

On the second night, Frannie found the energy to go back to the Volstead. Not many places threw away as much food as they did. This time, there were more scraps of beef, and even a half-full bottle of wine. On the third night, she found a few potatoes and a little whiskey left in a bottle. Frannie lamented this night. But it was all she had, so she drank the meager amount of whiskey, then went home to sleep.

On the fourth night, when she placed her hand on the tin can and lifted it, a booming woman's voice came from behind her. "What are ye doing there, Miss?"

Frannie dropped the garbage can lid and tried to run, but she tripped and fell.

"Wait, wait, missy," the woman said. She walked over. Frannie turned, looking up from the ground, her hand nervously covering her face. "I'm sorry!"

In a stern voice, the woman said, "Who are you?"

"I'm...Frannie."

The large woman only stared. Then she asked, "What are ye doing here?"

Frannie's voice trembled. "I'm…looking for food."

The woman reached down and helped her stand. "Have ye none?"

"No. My husband is dead. I have no one."

The woman looked over at the can and was quiet for a moment. Then she said, "My name is Rosie, but they call me Big Rosie. I run this place. I've a room downstairs in the basement. Come in tonight and stay here. I will fix ye somethin' to eat."

"I can't… " Frannie said. "I have to go home."

"It sounds like ye have no one at home, and it looks like yer starvin'. Now I insist. Come with me, lass. Tomorrow you and I can have a talk."

Frannie felt so tired. She realized she had no better option. "Okay."

And that was how she first came to know Rosie. Frannie smiled, turning her attention again to the Christmas music playing softly at the hardware store across the street.

Just then, a small yellow bird landed on her windowsill. Frannie thought it odd, as birds like this were not around on cold, overcast, wintry December mornings. She wondered if perhaps it was a sign that everything would be okay.

~ ~ ~ ~

A knock on the door woke Jake from his slumber. He lifted his head, then glanced at the clock. It was only 8:15 in the morning.

"Who is it?" a groggy Jake mumbled.

"It's Big Rosie."

"One minute," Jake replied, hustling out of bed.

He fixed himself up quickly, putting on his shoes and tucking in his shirt, then walked over and opened the door, smiling. "Good morning, Big Rosie."

"Good morning, Mr. Butterfield. I was stopping to see how you are doing." She peered over his shoulder, looking into his room.

"Come in," Jake said.

"Rosie walked in, scanning the room nonchalantly. "I see you are doing better."

"I am. And thanks for talking with me the other day."

Big Rosie nodded. "I am happy you heard me. You come from good stock, Jake Butterfield."

"I do. Thank you."

They were quiet for a moment, until Rosie said, "Well, I ought to be going." She turned to leave but scanned the room once more, her gaze landing on him. With a nod, she turned and left.

Jake smiled, unsure of what to say. He watched her go down the hall and knock on Frannie's door. Then he closed his own door and exhaled loudly.

~ ~ ~ ~

It was another cold, overcast Friday morning as Jake drove his snow-covered Impala over to the Port Sandusky Restaurant, where he bought breakfast and a coffee to go.

It was almost noon when he pulled onto an old country road that was aptly named Old Railroad Road. Jake fumbled with the paper he'd written the address on, then drove until he reached the first mailbox with a house number on it. He kept going. The houses were spaced pretty far apart; Jake estimated a quarter mile between each. The second mailbox seemed to be in disrepair. But there it was: 2500 Old Railroad Road.

Jake peered out his front windshield at the house. It had old wooden siding with peeling light blue paint. Wide stone steps led up to a large front porch. A white screen door flapped in the wind. Jake turned up the slight incline, his tires crunching the untouched snow of the driveway. He stopped and got out. He went to his trunk, got out a flathead screwdriver, put it in his coat pocket, and then turned to look at the path to the porch. His shoes crunched the frozen top layer of the snow as he crossed the large snow-covered lawn.

He finally reached the steps. He took the key from his pocket and jiggled it in the lock before opening the old wooden door.

Jake took a step inside and shook the snow from his shoes. He was in the middle of a long living room, one time seemed to have forgotten. The floors were wood, and the walls were thick plaster, painted a light yellow. A maroon paisley circular rug was in the middle. Two modest couches, old but clean looking, adorned each wall. At the end of the room was a brick fireplace with a stone mantel.

A large picture window offered a beautiful view of the road and the snow-covered fields beyond. Jake imagined his relatives who had lived here being very happy in this place.

He went into the dining room and sat at the table for a moment, looking at the view out the back window, which offered a view of even more fields and a clear view of a creek that ran through the property. Jake thought a person could find profound peace out here.

He wondered why Wayne had said it was in such disrepair. Jake was no expert in houses, but this didn't seem too far gone. Of course, he had not gone down into the basement—nor would he.

He found the stairs and made his way up to the largest bedroom. He figured this was the room the letter had referred to. He went to the closet, opened it, knelt down, and started pressing on the wooden floorboards. One was loose. He pried it up, and there before him was a handkerchief. Jake took it out and unfurled it. A gold watch was inside. He looked down at the hole again and saw a small pouch—it contained five small pieces of gold. "Wow," Jake said aloud.

He went back down to the living room and sat on the couch, looking at the items in his hand. They had been stuck in time. His own life was stuck in time. His marriage was stuck, maybe over. His writing career, which had once held promise, was stuck. He himself was stuck.

He was glad he had come. Before he left, he glanced around one more time. Then he locked the front door and started for his car. To his left, on the other side of the driveway, toward the wood line, was an old cemetery. It looked like an old-fashioned family cemetery, with not many graves.

As he walked toward it, he counted eleven gravestones. As he got closer, he glanced at each of the stones. All of them were snow-covered, and most were so old they were unreadable. He could make out the name Butterfield on a few. Jake realized these were some of his ancestors.

He saw three gravestones closest to the gate, as if set off by themselves. Jake walked over and brushed the snow off the marble stones.

One read Captain Bradley Butterfield.

"Wow!" Jake exclaimed. "I thought he'd have been buried in Gettysburg, but Sal was right. They must have brought him back."

Jake turned to look at the house again, thinking of the captain living there long before he had gone to war. He turned to look at the next grave and glanced at his watch. It was getting late. He brushed the snow off the barely readable gravestone.

It belonged to a baby.

He started to step over to the final grave when a fierce gust of wind blew icy snow onto his already cold face. Jake grimaced.

At the same time, he heard the sound of tires crunching the frozen snow and turned to see a large black Buick Electra pull into the drive behind him. A rather tall man got out. Jake recognized him. It was the man he had seen at the library.

"You there," the man said. There was a broad smile on his face as he got out of the car, holding his trench coat closed. The man approached. "My name is Bixby, Mr. Bixby. I am from a family of the town founders, and I happened to see you turn down this road. I understand you are one of the Butterfields?"

"Yes, hi. My name is Jake Butterfield."

"Nice to meet you, Mr. Butterfield. So, I hear you are selling the place," Mr. Bixby said.

"Yes, I am."

Mr. Bixby looked over at the house, shaking his head. "It's in terrible shape. Some say it's cursed. If I were you, I would sell and get going while the going is good."

"Well, that is what I plan to do. The day after Christmas, I hope."

"Oh, that sounds good. You're lucky to get rid of it. It's in such bad shape." Bixby looked toward the house again, this time with a grimace.

"It's not really that bad. At least, not as bad as I thought," said Jake.

"Hmmm. Well, best of luck to you, Mr. Butterfield. It was nice to meet you."

"You too, Mr. Bixby."

Mr. Bixby strutted to his car, seeming oblivious to the icy conditions. He got in, pulled out of the driveway, and sped off with one final smile.

Jake felt another blast of wind. He bowed his head quickly, then went to his car and backed down the icy driveway.

As he drove back into town, he caught a glimpse of a large woman with a black knee-length coat and a winter hat and scarf trudging down the opposite side of the street. Jake slowed and looked over his shoulder. It was Big Rosie. *I wonder where she's going,* he thought.

He turned around, waited for her to turn the corner, then slowly followed her as she hustled across the street toward St. Mary's Church. Jake watched her go up the steps and into the old church.

"Well, good for Big Rosie."

Jake thought about going in. He was Catholic, though it had been at least ten years since he'd been to church. He turned his car toward the Volstead instead.

It was 4:00 p.m. when he said hello to Sal.

"Coffee, Jake?" Sal asked.

"Yes, and can I get one of your famous ham sandwiches?"

"I picked some up today, just for you. I also picked up some fresh turkey. Would you like to try one of those too?"

"You know what, Sal? I am famished. Go ahead and make me one of each."

Sal went into the back. He returned shortly with the sandwiches. "So did you find anything out by going back to the old house, Jake?"

"No, not really. There's an old graveyard out there. And you are right: Captain Butterfield is buried there, but I didn't get a chance to look through it too much. It was too cold."

"Yeah, it's a cold one," Sal said. "I thought Captain Butterfield was buried there, along with someone who used to live out there, or lived there for a while…"

"Hmmm, interesting," Jake said, sipping his hot coffee. "It's a small town."

"Yeah, you can say that again."

"Well, here's some money for the sandwiches. Thanks for thinking of me today. I'm going upstairs."

"Sounds good, Jake. Tomorrow is Christmas Eve. We'll be open until the early evening."

"Great. Good to know," said Jake.

Jake spent the rest of the night in his room. He took a hot shower and did some reading.

The Christmas music from the hardware store across the street proved to be soothing, and Jake slowly fell asleep.

Saturday

Christmas Eve

Mr. Bixby waited for the library to open. Then he went inside. He waited for the librarian to leave her desk, then went into the adjacent archive room. He already knew where the boxes were, and he went right to them and opened the second one. He was crossing a line, he knew, but it really was a gray area. He could not remove anything; however, technically, he could move things around a bit. He dug down toward the bottom of the box and picked up the last letter. He opened it slightly, smiled, then tucked it neatly onto a shelf.

He heard a noise behind him and slowly turned. There was no one there. He sighed and peered out to the front desk. The librarian had not returned. He thought about moving more letters, but he could not take the chance. He might be noticed. He thought for a moment, considering whether he should do more. No, this would suffice. The key to the puzzle had been hidden. That was his business, after all. Keeping things hidden. Keeping the truth hidden.

~ ~ ~ ~

Jake got his things and headed back to the library to continue his research. When he walked in, Diane, the librarian, was at the desk.

"Good morning, Mr. Butterfield."

"Oh, hi. I'm sorry. I forgot your name."

"That's no problem. I'm sure you have met a lot of new people in this town. My name is Diane. You are early today," she remarked, with a kind smile.

"Yes, I wanted to continue looking through the archives."

"No problem. I will get them for you." She pushed her glasses up on her nose and said, "We have special hours today."

"Oh, what are they?"

"We close at 3:00, since it's Christmas Eve."

"Okay, great. Thank you."

Jake went to the adjoining room.

Moments later, Diane returned with the two boxes. Jake sifted through them until he found three letters folded up and grouped together between two books. He carefully separated them and unfolded the first. It was from Captain Butterfield's wife to Jake's Great-Grandfather Archibald.

Dear Archibald,

Have you heard anything about your brother Bradley? He has been missing for so long, and I am losing hope that he will come home to me. Our baby has been ill, and I am overwhelmed at the thought of losing both of them. I have no one else in this world. Please let me know what you find.

Sincerely,
Marie Francis Butterfield

Jake shook his head. "The poor girl. All alone." The other letter which was attached to it seemed to signify it was a response to the first. It was his Great Grandfather Archibald's reply.

Dear Marie,

We have not heard anything about Bradley. Many are still missing. Most of them, I fear, are dead. But we hold on to hope. It is impossible for us to get to you because of the war.

Sincerely,
Archibald Butterfield

Jake pulled out the final letter in the group, written just one month later.

Dear Archibald,

My baby has died. His fever grew too much for him to bear. We had the doctor here, but there was nothing he could do. I now fear I am alone in this world. I don't know how I will be able to go on, because all the people I love are dead.

Sincerely,
Marie Francis Butterfield

Jake shook his head and said aloud, "This story just keeps getting sadder and sadder." He wiped a tear from his eye. Stories like this always touched him.

He stood up and walked around the library, collecting his thoughts. After a while, he returned to the archives and opened the last box. Several books were on top, with a letter between the first two. It was dated three months later and addressed to his Great Grandfather Archibald.

When he glanced at the long letter's signature, his eyes widened. It was from Captain Butterfield. Jake's mind began to race. *But I thought he was dead. How could he have written a letter after he died at Gettysburg? Jake wasted no more time. With a furrowed brow, he read voraciously.*

February 19, 1864
Marietta, Ohio

To: Major Archibald Butterfield
34th Regiment
Louisville, Kentucky

Dear Archibald,

I rejoice to tell you I have escaped Libby Prison. I have been granted a furlough for one month, and I am returning home to see my beloved wife and infant son.

I long to see you again, brother.

At Gettysburg, I was wounded. Shot in the arm. Most of my unit perished. The Rebs took three of my men and me prisoner on July 2. There was no way to get word to anyone about what happened to us. I heard that I had been listed among the missing. I loathe the fact that I could not save my men from capture. I was their leader, and I failed them.

It took two weeks to march with Lee's army to Richmond, Virginia, where we were put into Libby Prison. The conditions were beyond horrible. In the first few months, many men died of disease. But after some time of hopelessness, hope came to us, for we became determined to escape.

Colonel Thomas Rose led our efforts to escape. We were all housed in a large, four-story abandoned warehouse. In the basement was an old kitchen that had become infested with rats. The Rebs called it Rat Hell. They never went down there.

Colonel Rose found a way to get behind a wall on the second floor and into an abandoned chimney, which took us right to the middle of Rat Hell.

Down in the old kitchen, we started to dig a tunnel. There were seventeen of us who worked three shifts, around the clock, slipping down the chimney into Rat Hell to take our turn digging the tunnel. It was the darkest place I have ever been. The sounds and feel of hundreds of rats scurrying about us and on top of us will always haunt me.

But those little varmints were our saviors. The Rebs hated the rats so much that they never stepped into Rat Hell, and that gave us the cover we needed.

It took eighteen days to dig our tunnel. Midway through the eighteenth day, we surfaced on the other side of a tobacco warehouse outside the camp. There, we made our plan. That night, we began the exodus.

We left six at a time, spacing ourselves out. One hundred and nine of us made it out before the Rebs discovered the break. Sadly, we did not all make it to the Union lines. Two of my men were recaptured. But fifty-nine of the one hundred and nine who escaped made it home.

I am now a few more days of travel away from seeing my beloved Marie and our little son. I cannot wait to surprise her.

Your Brother,
Captain Bradley Butterfield.

"Holy mackerel," Jake exclaimed to himself. He bolted up, his heart racing, his eyes wide with excitement. He looked around the library, wanting to share his discovery—but there was no one there. He said aloud, "Captain Bradley Butterfield did not die at Gettysburg like his wife thought. That's why he is buried at the house."

Jake felt a wave of satisfaction run over him. The writer in him, the researcher, the pursuer of clues, was back in action. For the first time in a long time, he felt good about himself. He felt even more enthusiastic about going back to see the graves again tomorrow. He needed to see them. Maybe there would be a happy ending for the family after all.

He sat back down, shaking his head in disbelief at all he had uncovered.

~ ~ ~ ~

Father Tom put on his black overcoat, buttoned it up, and pulled the top collars together to block the wind from hitting his neck. The skies were beginning to darken ever so slowly. The great feast of Christmas would in just a few hours.

Sunset marked the start of Christmas Eve. That was when the magic of the night began its descent upon the earth, just as it had done since that very first night, when the Angels descended and made the great announcement to the shepherds.

Father Tom never tired of recalling their magical words from that magical night. The shepherds were afraid, but the lead Angel said to them, "Do not be afraid; for behold, I proclaim to you good news of great joy that will be for all the people. For today in the city of David a savior has been born for you who is Messiah and Lord. And this will be a sign for you: you will find an infant wrapped in swaddling clothes and lying in a manger."

And then the rest of the Angels proclaimed the age-old truth of God's desire to help humanity: "Glory to God in the highest and on earth peace to those on whom his favor rests."

Father Tom smiled broadly. He thought about all the people he was assigned to care for. Many who were struggling in life, many who faced unseen adversaries, and he whispered a prayer that on this night they would feel God's presence and would feel his favor in their lives.

He reached the back door of the library and went in. As he strolled through, he noticed a few patrons quietly reading. He saw the librarian at the front desk, hard at work. He passed down the hall behind her and decided to head to the archive room. Then he stopped.

Not far away was someone he really despised. By his very nature and station in life, he was not supposed to despise anyone, for everyone had potential—potential to change, potential to abandon their ways should those ways be contrary to what was good. But Mr. Bixby was standing in the doorway, peering into the archive room.

Father Tom walked up behind him. "Mr. Bixby."

Bixby slowly straightened, then turned. "Oh, if it isn't Father Tom. Fancy meeting you here."

"Yes, it is quite the coincidence. What brings you here, Mr. Bixby?"

"Oh, just looking through some books."

"You wouldn't be trying to cause any trouble now, would you?"

"Oh, you know me, Father Tom. I stay about my business no matter the season."

Father Tom nodded glumly. He did not understand the likes of Bixby. Why did they persist in causing trouble? What, really, would they ever gain? The truth was: nothing.

Father Tom glanced out a nearby window. "Speaking of seasons, Christmas Eve is upon us. Don't you have somewhere else you need to be?"

Bixby's face narrowed, and a look of disdain quickly crossed it. Then it relaxed, and ever so slowly a manufactured smile appeared. "Yes, I do have to go soon. But I will be back."

"Very well. You better get going."

Bixby tipped his hat, then started to walk around Father Tom. Father Tom considered him, then said, "Christmas Eve Mass will begin soon. Are you sure you don't want to come this year?"

Bixby stopped, turned, and glared. "That is the last place I would want to be. Good day, Father."

Father Tom watched him leave and then felt a sense of worry. What was Bixby up to, and why had he been there? Father Tom walked over to the wing adjacent to the archive room. Jake was at the table, engrossed in some manuscript. "Hello again, Jake."

Jake read one more line intently, then looked up wide-eyed. "Oh, hello, Father Tom. How are you?"

"I am well. Are you coming to Christmas Eve Mass this evening?"

"Well, I am not sure."

"Well, consider yourself invited."

"Thank you, Father. I will see." Jake was not so sure he was ready to go to church. But he felt a genuine warmth coming from the priest. It felt like days of old, when he was a child and his mother had taken him to church.

Father Tom said, "I'll be up at the front desk, in case you're checking anything out. I'm locking up today so Diane our librarian can go home early."

Jake glanced at his watch. It was nearly 3:00 p.m. The library would be closing soon.

Father Tom smiled, then turned and walked out. Jake watched him, nodding slowly. The man had a wonderful presence about him, not only in the gentle way he spoke, but also in the even-keeled way he walked. Jake looked down at the remaining letters and glanced at the time again. He would have to return after Christmas to review the rest, since the library would be closed. Perhaps he would come early on Monday, or even after the appointment with Mr. Pearsall to sign the final papers for the house sale.

~ ~ ~ ~

Jake strolled down the main thoroughfare back toward the Volstead. Christmas Eve was descending fast, and one could feel the excitement growing. Shops were busy; people were bustling along the sidewalk, and Christmas music was playing. The faint hint of dusk descending was in the air, which turned the focus to the Christmas lights and displays beckoning from shop windows. The old, desolate town Jake had driven into just seven days earlier was alive with life and lights.

But it wasn't just the town: it was himself. Jake felt alive too, and, more importantly, free. The old writer's wheels in his mind had begun to turn again. His sunken opinion of himself was changing. Discovering that his great-grandfather had been in the Civil War intrigued him. Finding out that Captain Butterfield did not die at Gettysburg but, rather, escaped from a POW camp and came back to Sandusky also intrigued him. The writer in him, the investigator and researcher, was coming back to life. He could not wait to return to the Volstead and tell Sal what he had learned.

As he turned the corner, Jake saw the Old Ironside Bar. He hesitated for a moment, but then kept walking. As he drew closer, he started to feel a tightness in his chest. His footsteps slowed. He could practically feel the warm vibrations coming from inside the bar. Patrons were celebrating the holiday, laughing and talking with beers in hand and drinks on tables in front of them.

Jake stopped on the sidewalk and looked inside, thinking. It might not hurt to have one drink. It could be a gift, his own Christmas gift to himself, for working so hard on his research and coming into a lot of money once the place was sold.

But as he reached for the door handle, Big Rosie came to mind, and something made him stop. He felt a shudder, a warning. He could see her furrowed brow and her eyes glaring at him. But it was not only that. He had promised her, and this was a promise he could not go back on. He was not going to disappoint her.

Jake removed his hand from the door handle and lowered his arm. He turned away from the door with all his might and slowly stepped down the sidewalk, back toward the Volstead. His eyes were half-closed and his breathing heavy, blowing clouds into the cold, crisp air. As he walked, he tried to understand why he had felt enough power to walk away from the bar—after all, he had broken promises before, but this one felt different.

Finally, he reached the front door of the Volstead and went in.

"Hello there, Jake," came the friendly, familiar voice.

"Oh, hi, Sal," Jake said.

"I've got a fresh pot of coffee and some fresh ham in back waiting for you."

"Great," Jake said excitedly. "I have a few things to tell you anyway."

Sal smiled broadly and turned his hat from the back to the front as he said, "Sit down right here, Jake. I'll get you all squared away."

Within moments, Jake had a piping hot cup of coffee in front of him and an overflowing ham sandwich on a white plate next to it. Sal had garnished the plate with chips today.

Jake smiled, sipped his coffee, put some mustard on his sandwich, and took a bite. "Sal, you've been really good to me. I could get used to this place."

"Ah, it's no trouble, Jake. You'd do the same for me."

Jake nodded. "I would."

"So, what did you find out at the library, Jake?"

Jake smiled, nodding. "Well, for starters, Captain Butterfield did not die at Gettysburg. He escaped from a POW camp and came back here to Sandusky. That's why he's buried here. I am going to try to find out more after Christmas."

"Well, I'll be a monkey's uncle," Sal replied, shaking his head, his eyes full of wonder. "How did he die?"

"Well, I don't know that yet. The library opens back up Monday morning. I'll see what else I can find out. What time is it anyway, Sal?"

"It's getting close to 4:30."

Jake looked outside. Dusk was beginning its wintery descent. It would be dark soon. "I can't believe how dark it gets this time of year up here, Sal."

"Yes," Sal said, turning to look out the front window. "It does, indeed. I like it, though, with the Christmas lights and all. It gives our lives an air of mystery."

Both men looked out the front window. The Christmas music from the hardware store across the street was playing faintly through the glass, and the Christmas lights twinkled as if they knew a secret.

"I'll be closing up for a little while soon, but I'll reopen about 6:30," Sal said.

"Oh." Jake looked puzzled. Usually, the bar was open for a few more hours.

Sal said, "I'm going to Christmas Eve Mass at 5:00. You should come, Jake."

Jake smiled and looked outside again. The Christmas music had put him in an olden-days, Christmassy mood. Going to Mass might be enjoyable.

"You know what, Sal? I'll go."

"Oh, that's great, Jake. My wife and I are always on the left side, not too many pews from the front. You can sit with us. We'll be looking for you."

"Okay. Thanks, Sal."

Jake threw down a few bucks and went upstairs to get ready. He was glad that this Christmas Eve, he would not be sitting at a bar with strangers, as he had so many years past.

~ ~ ~ ~

A little before 5:00 p.m., Jake strolled down to St. Mary's Church. The evening's dark blue clouds were the perfect backdrop to the Christmas lights. But it was more than just the lights. There was a solemness in the air, a feeling of mystery. Jake remembered his mother walking him to church as a child. He had not thought of her in a long time, and he smiled. She had told him that on Christmas Eve Angels came down from Heaven to dwell closely with Earth's men, women, and children. They were around other times, but not like they were on Christmas Eve. Because the Dark Angels were forbidden to be active on the Earth on Christmas Eve, the night felt all the more magical. It was as if Heaven, with all its goodness, unimpeded by forces of darkness, was present on Earth for one night each year.

Jake marveled at the thought. It had not occurred to him since he was a child, and yet tonight he felt it all, and he remembered what his mother had told him. A tear escaped his eye, running down his cheek, feeling cold on his face.

He neared the church and saw cars parking, dropping people off. Those already in the lot were lightly dusted with newly fallen snow. People and families were coming from all directions on foot, having walked from their nearby businesses or homes. It seemed like the whole town was on its way to the church.

Jake went inside.

The sight and sounds of the hundreds of people milling about surprised him. He had not been in any church in a long time. He ducked his way through the large vestibule and made his way to some broad wooden doors on the left. Jake went in and was greeted by another wave of people, who were standing just inside, quietly watching for loved ones or searching over the heads of those already seated.

Jake went up the aisle. He could hear the organist's soft Christmas instrumentals from above. He took his time, taking in the surroundings and the faces of so many warm hearts, excited for the great celebration of Christmas to commence.

He saw Sal standing in one of the front pews, right where he said he would be. Jake smiled and made his way over. Sal extended his hand. "Merry Christmas, Jake." He turned, leaning aside. "This is my wife, Sandy."

Sandy stood, hand extended. "Hi, Jake. I've heard a lot about you."

"Oh, you have?" Jake glanced at Sal and smiled. "It's nice to meet you, Sandy."

"Sit down, sit down," Sal said.

They sat, two rows from the front, and waited as the time drew nearer and the commotion began to die down. Soon, there was nothing but the quiet murmur of people waiting, leaning over and whispering to each other, as was the way in Catholic churches right before Mass began.

A bell rang, and everyone stood as the organist began to play "O Come, All Ye Faithful." Sal picked up from the first line, singing loudly, leading the little section of people in the front corner of the church. He nodded to Jake, signaling he should join in, and Jake promptly did, but quietly.

The priest, a taller man in his mid-seventies, with thick gray hair, came out with three servers and made his way to the altar to begin the liturgy. Jake relished the wonderful, warm energy in the church. It reminded him of attending church with his mother when he was very young. He had forgotten so much about those days, but tonight brought the feelings and memories back again.

Throughout the entire service, Jake marveled at the statues and décor adorning the front and side altars. The words of the liturgy, so often just background noise to him, had meaning tonight. It was as if he were hearing them for the first time. He was waking up inside, something he had not even realized he needed to do. His mind drifted to the last several years of his depression, and he realized that coming to Sandusky and meeting Sal, Big Rosie, Frannie, and all the others had been slowly pulling him out of it. He'd needed to come to this town more than he knew.

At the Sign of Peace, Jake turned and saw Big Rosie sitting in the last pew, in the corner. He wanted to greet her, but he knew it would have to wait until after the service. As everyone shook hands, Jake shook Sal's, then turned to watch Big Rosie, hoping to catch her attention. She was smiling, nodding at the people around her.

After Mass, Jake thanked Sal and his wife and went back to try to catch Big Rosie. When he got to her pew, she was gone. Father Tom was there, standing in the back. He was holding a book in his hands, smiling and nodding at the parishioners as they passed. He noticed Jake and walked over. "Good evening, Jake."

"Good evening, Father," Jake said, looking around. "I was looking for a friend of mine."

"Do you mean Big Rosie?"

Jake nodded, wondering how he knew.

Father Tom said, "Oh, she left a good bit ago."

"Oh, I see." Jake frowned, nodding. "You know her, Father?"

"Of course, I do. I am a friend of Big Rosie's. She is one of my favorite people."

Jake looked up. "Mine, too, Father. She's made, uh…quite an impression on me."

"That's Rosie's way," Father Tom said matter-of-factly. "It's always been her way."

"Have you known her long?" Jake asked.

"Yes, it seems a very long time. We go back a long way. So, how did you make out at the library today?"

"I found out some great stuff. That's a really nice place."

"Yes, it is," Father Tom said. "Well, what are you doing tomorrow for Christmas Day?"

"I'll probably lay low, maybe go out to get a bite to eat. How about you, Father?"

"I have the 8:00 a.m. Christmas Day Mass, and then I will probably have breakfast and write some letters to family members. A quiet day for me too."

Jake nodded. "Well, Merry Christmas, Father Tom."

"Aye, Jake," Father Tom replied with a touch of an Irish accent.

Jake thought it strange that the priest had suddenly spoken with an Irish accent, one that sounded much like Big Rosie's, but he didn't mention it.

"Oh, Jake?" Father Tom called out.

Jake turned. "Yes, Father?"

"You know, you never had time to go through that last box."

"Oh, yes, I plan to. Um, what time does the library open on Monday?"

"Come over and see me at the rectory at 7:00 a.m. in the morning on Monday. If I am free, I will open it up for you."

"Thank you," Jake said.

"Good night, Jake. Merry Christmas to you."

Jake turned to leave, then glanced over his shoulder. The priest was already gone. Jake scanned the aisles, expecting to see him. Then he shook his head and went out the door to head back to the Volstead. Everything was falling into place perfectly.

~ ~ ~ ~

When Jake arrived back at the Volstead, the bar was crowded. Jake had never seen it so alive with people. Sal was back behind the bar. His wife Sandy was sitting at one of the tables with a woman Jake had never seen. Sal still had on his church clothes, and he looked especially prominent behind the bar dressed so nicely. His hat was turned backward, as it was when he was busy. He hustled up some beverages for those who had just come in. Sal smiled. "Come in and join us, Jake. I saved your favorite seat."

Jake sat down. It was the only seat left in the crowded bar. Sal came over and said, "Jake, I already fixed you another sandwich. I will grab it in a moment. I have some chips too."

"That would be great, Sal."

"One fresh coffee and a ham sandwich coming right up." He returned momentarily with a piping hot cup of coffee and set it in front of Jake.

"Thanks, Sal. I really appreciate all this," Jake said over the bar's noise. The place now held about thirty people and was noisier than Jake had ever heard it.

Sal said, "I'm proud of you, Jake. Cutting back on drinking and all. I can tell you're a good man, and it's a good thing you are doing."

"Well, you can thank Big Rosie for that."

Sal chuckled, then turned his cap around to the front.

"Well, you're not the first person who claimed to have had help from Big Rosie."

Jake took a sip of his coffee, half smiling. "She owns the place, right?"

"Well, she used to, I guess. But that was quite a—" Sal stopped mid-sentence and looked up. The front door opened, and in walked Mr. Gill. "Hello, Mr. Gill," Sal exclaimed. "One second, Jake."

Mr. Gill ushered his wife in, and with a sweep of his hand said aloud, "Hello to you, good men and women of the Volstead. I come bearing good tidings. Merry Christmas to you all. A round of drinks for everyone, Sal."

"Merry Christmas," came the collective cry, and the noise and holiday cheer resumed.

Jake turned back to Sal, who was busy getting everyone their drinks. Two other couples came in, and with the round of drinks being poured and the new customers, there was no way Jake could get Sal's attention. He decided to go to his room.

~ ~ ~ ~

Jake strolled across the old wooden floor and up the rickety staircase that led to the rooms upstairs. As he walked past Big Rosie's room, he saw light coming from under the door. He walked slowly, careful to not stop but slow enough to listen. She was humming. Jake imagined her sitting in front of her Christmas tree. He smiled and continued to his room.

No sooner had he shut his door when he froze. Something was bothering him, something Sal had said. It didn't make any sense. He felt a rush of adrenaline race through him. The writer, the journalist within him, was stirring. He set his sandwich down, looked in the mirror, and straightened his hair. He needed to find out more about Big Rosie. Who was she really? He walked to Big Rosie's room and knocked.

The humming stopped, followed by silence. Jake knocked gently again, calling out, "Rosie?"

He heard a chair move, then the sound of footsteps crossing the long wooden floor toward the door. Jake's palms began to sweat. Something about this entire moment felt off. He realized though, despite her authoritative demeanor, Big Rosie had been nothing but honest and kind. He waited for the door to open, and when it did, he quickly gathered himself.

There she was, Big Rosie, smiling wide at him with her Irish eyes. She said in her thick Irish accent, "Hello, Mr. Butterfield. What are ye doing this Christmas Eve?"

"Hi, Rosie—I mean, Big Rosie. I, uh, well, I was just going to say hi to you."

"Aye, that's awful nice of ye to check on me. Come in, and call me Rosie, Mr. Butterfield."

Jake swallowed and walked past her. The room was like his in many ways, but it was bare. It was a single square room with wooden floors. On the wall was a large antique mirror. There was also a kitchenette area and a simple wooden bed—old, like his. A gas lamp sat upon on the dresser, lighting the dresser and bed area. There was one in the kitchen too, turned low but giving light to the small, circular wooden table. In the center of the living area was a chair on either side of a Christmas tree, which was no more than five feet tall. Next to each chair was a small wooden table. A candle burned on each one. The tree was decorated with old-fashioned ornaments. No lights, just ornaments.

The entire room felt like Christmas, like Christmas past.

Rosie motioned to the chair. "Please sit down, Mr. Butterfield."

Jake walked past the mirror, admiring the warm reflection of the tree it held. "Thank you," he said as he sat. He glanced out the window, which looked out the side of the Volstead and toward the distant street.

"O Little Town of Bethlehem" was playing from the hardware store speaker. It was soothing sitting there with Rosie. It felt like an energy was transferring between them—not like when she'd chastised him. This felt more like a tranquilly drifting raft on a quiet lake.

Rosie sat, her smile tight-lipped, her glasses resting peacefully on her nose. Her brownish gray hair was pulled back, and in the candlelight her fair skin glowed. She had on the dress she normally wore, her thick-heeled shoes resting steady on the floor.

Neither of them said a word.

Then Jake cleared his throat. "I saw you at the Christmas Eve Mass."

"Aye, I was there."

"It was a nice service," Jake said, trying to make small talk.

Rosie said, "Aye, and it was nice seeing two priests on the altar. We don't get to see that too often these days."

Jake squinted slightly. "Oh, were there two?"

"Well, of course. Father Manning and Father Tom."

Jake was puzzled. Hi thought that only Father Manning had presided over the Mass. He must have missed seeing Father Tom. Jake changed the subject. "I met Father Tom after Mass. He said he knows you very well."

Big Rosie smiled and bowed her head. "He's been a good friend to me for a long time."

Jake nodded. "He said that. He seems very nice."

"Aye, he is," Rosie said. There was quiet for a while as Jake glanced over, watching Big Rosie, who was mesmerized by the tree, tapping her foot to some silent rhythm. Her thoughts seemed far away.

"Rosie, have you lived here long?"

"Yes, for a long time now. I'm getting old, though, so I don't know how much longer I'll be."

Jake nodded, smiling. "So, you and Frannie are friends?"

"We've been together through a lot, Mr. Butterfield. Frannie has been at my side for a very long time. She is almost like a daughter to me now. I could never leave her behind."

"I see," Jake said. "Frannie seems to like it here."

Big Rosie started to say something but then paused before continuing, "Mr. Butterfield, sometimes a person can regret something with all their heart and soul, and it can trap them, keep them, and they don't know how to move on. After a while, they may not even remember what happened if they are unwilling to face it." She drifted off, her gaze falling on the Christmas tree.

Jake felt confused.

There was a knock at the door. Jake jumped, but Big Rosie nodded, as if to say, "It's okay." She got up and opened the door.

Frannie walked in. "Oh, my goodness Rosie. You have company. I'm sorry." She blushed and looked down.

Jake stood, folding his hands in front of himself, trying to appear as gentle as possible. He said, "It's okay, Frannie. You can join us."

Rosie added, "Aye, Frannie. I'll get ye a chair."

Rosie took the last chair from her kitchenette and sat it in the middle, so all three could face the tree. The music gently continued from across the street, making the entire moment feel like Christmas.

Frannie sat with her hands folded, rocking gently. She smiled at Jake, then at Rosie. Her hair looked stunning in the candlelight. It hung down her shoulders. Jake could see the candlelight flickering in her beautiful, big brown eyes. She, too, wore the same dress Jake had always seen her wear around the place.

"It's almost Christmas again, Rosie," Frannie said, as if Jake were not there.

"Aye, Frannie. It is."

Frannie nodded. "I hope it will be a Merry Christmas for us."

"Aye, it will, Frannie," Rosie said.

Jake was amazed at how time seemed to stand still. He wanted to say more but felt content to watch the candlelight reflections flicker in the ornaments of the Christmas tree. Outside, "Silent Night" began to play, and Jake noticed fresh snowflakes dropping. It all felt magical, surreal, even sacred, and he did not know why.

"Have you worked here long, Frannie?" Jake asked as he turned to her.

"I've been here as long as Rosie has almost."

"Do you like it here?"

"Why sure," she said, smiling gently, turning her eyes from the tree to Jake. "I have no choice but to stay here, Mr. Butterfield. Rosie has been so good to me."

"Oh, I see," Jake said. "Would you ever leave to work elsewhere, Frannie?" He glanced over at Rosie, but she only stared into the tree.

Frannie closed her eyes, and her smile wavered ever so slightly. "I have nowhere else to go, Mr. Butterfield. There was a great misunderstanding in my life. It is here I must stay."

Rosie patted her knee. "You'll be all right, Frannie. Don't worry."

Jake wondered about her choice of words. What did she mean? All their words seemed odd to him.

Rosie interrupted his thoughts. "It's time for us to turn in now, Mr. Butterfield."

"Oh, yes, sure," Jake said. He looked at his watch. It was nearly 7:30. He stood up slowly, saying, "I wish you both a Merry Christmas and a good night."

Rosie said, "Merry Christmas to you, Mr. Butterfield."

Jake smiled and walked to the door slowly. His reflection in the large antique mirror caught his eye, and he beheld the tree and chairs as he had when he walked in. He paused momentarily; something still felt off. But his attention was drawn back to the women as Frannie called out, "Merry Christmas, Mr. Butterfield."

"Merry Christmas, Frannie," he said, opening the door and returning to his room.

~ ~ ~ ~

Jake lay in bed thinking of the day, thinking of Christmas Eve in his past, listening to the music from the hardware store. He thought of his wife. They had special Christmas Eve's together, though it had been many years since the last meaningful one. He wished things might be different. Before long, he was fast asleep.

~ ~ ~ ~

Mr. Bixby cringed as he paced back and forth across his living quarters atop the abandoned Methodist church. He could not leave, and it made him feel like he was suffocating. He hated Christmas Eve, and Christmas Day more than any other day or night of the year.

Below him, the town of Sandusky was silent. Bixby hated the silence. It reminded him of the agony he had endured long ago, when he was imprisoned in a dark place. It was the longest five years of his life, each day feeling like an eternity. It had changed him. It had taken from him the final glimmer of light that his soul possessed.

He could not do anything this night, nor tomorrow. Rules were rules and he had to follow them, just like everyone else. Still. "Dammit!" he screamed, thrusting his fist against the wall. Events below were spinning out of his control and there was nothing he could do.

He began to try to talk out loud, hoping it might calm him down. "Calm down, Mr. Bixby. This happens every year, and it always works out."

Saying it aloud did not make him feel any better.

Long ago, someone had gotten in the way and caused him to fail. It was one of the reasons he was here so long. Who could have done it? One face appeared in his mind. He pounded his fist again against the wall again. "I will make him pay."

Sunday

Christmas Day

The End of It

At 7:43 a.m. on Christmas morning, Jake bolted up to a sitting position. It had been a long night of tormented sleep. Sal's words about Big Rosie had unsettled him. All night his mind had been trying to subconsciously work it out. He wished he had not left the bar before clarifying what Sal meant, but there was nothing he could do now. Sal was home for Christmas and would not be back until tomorrow morning.

Jake got up and walked to the chair by the window. The streets below were eerily quiet as they would be this early on any Christmas morning. It was not only Sal's words that had unsettled him. His conversation with Rosie and Frannie had also unsettled him. He went over the entire conversation with Rosie and Frannie hoping that by going through it slowly, he could figure out what was bothering him.

He looked across the room at his reflection in the mirror. Suddenly, it hit him. He stood up slowly, looking at his reflection, and walked ever so slowly toward the mirror, piecing it together. It was the mirror. He shuddered. Was he crazy? Was this even possible?

He paused, thinking. He needed to find out. He put his hands on his head, as his plan shaped up. *The library! Yes, the library. It might very well have something about the history of the Volstead. And... and Father Tom has the key.* He looked at his watch, and quickly got dressed. There was still time to catch him.

~ ~ ~ ~

Jake crept as quietly as he could down the hall, away from Rosie's room, past Frannie's room, and tiptoed down the back stairs. He checked his watch—8:20 a.m. Father Tom would be finished with Christmas Morning Mass soon.

Jake hustled over to the church and went in. He stood in the back, watching the morning mass finish. Only the pastor, Father Manning, was on the altar. The church was not as crowded as it had been the previous night, but the music and energy were the same. It was Christmas morning, and this was a shining moment in every church throughout the world.

Soon, the closing song was sung, the people were dismissed, and the gradual exit and glad greetings of parishioners began. Jake looked around, watching for Father Tom. Finally, he saw him walking down the aisle. Jake waved, and Father Tom came over.

"Good morning, Jake. Merry Christmas."

"Merry Christmas to you, Father Tom. May I speak to you?"

"Why, sure," Father Tom said. He stepped toward the back of the vestibule. "What can I do for you, Jake?"

Jake said, "I need your help."

"Sure, with what?"

Jake asked, "Do you have anything in the library about the history of the Volstead?"

"Yes, there is… Hmm, let me think. There is a book about its history. And we have some archived articles too, now that I think about it."

"Father, is there any way you could let me in there this morning?"

"On Christmas morning? It can't wait until Monday, like we talked about?"

"Father, it is really important. I…um… I can't explain it."

"Don't worry a bit, Jake." Father Tom paused, thinking, his brow furrowed. Then he glanced to his right, raised his hand, and called out, "Ginny?"

Jake turned. An older lady with frail hands and two long grayish-black braids walked over. She was wearing a plaid dress and carrying a cane. "Good morning, Father. Merry Christmas."

Father Tom gestured to Jake. "Ginny, this is Mr. Butterfield."

"Hello, Mr. Butterfield," Ginny said, smiling. "Merry Christmas to you."

Jake smiled, nodding hurriedly. Then he considered Ginny. "Oh, yes. You brought the lost box to the counter for me the other day."

Ginny nodded.

Father Tom said, "Ginny helps me out around the parish and over at the library on occasion." He turned. "Ginny, can you meet me at the library in about fifteen minutes? Mr. Butterfield needs something from the archives."

"Today?" Ginny looked up at Father Tom quizzically.

Father Tom nodded. "I know, Ginny, I know. But don't worry. As a trustee, I can authorize it." He turned to Jake. "How long will you need?"

"Oh, a half hour or so," Jake said.

"I'd be happy to help," Ginny said. "A friend of Rosie's is a friend of mine."

Jake looked at her in surprise. "You know Big Rosie too?"

"Well, sure I do. I talk to her almost every day."

"Great," Father Tom said. "Jake, sit here in the back row. I'll go take care of a few final matters, then I'll grab the keys for the library."

~ ~ ~ ~

Father Tom, Jake, and Ginny walked out of the church, across the street, and over to the library's side door. Father Tom opened the door and held it while Jake and Ginny walked in and up the few steps. Father Tom said, "I have a few more things to wrap up at the church. I'll be back soon."

Jake was struck by how eerily silent the place was. Ginny interrupted his thoughts, saying, "Just a minute; I will turn on the lights."

Ginny disappeared, and soon the lights were on. Then she returned smiling and asked, "What would you like to see first, Jake?"

"Something about the history of the Volstead."

"Oh, I know just the book." She smiled widely, staring at him as if she were frozen. Jake thought she might be awaiting a response, so he awkwardly said, "Perfect."

At the word, Ginny nodded and turned. Jake followed her through the main lobby and into one of the wings. Ginny perused a long shelf of books, eyeing each one, moving to the next, then down and back over. She did this again and again, until she finally announced, "Here it is."

She pulled down a very old-looking book. In gold leaf was the title: *The Assorted and Sordid History of the Volstead Brothel*. She placed it in Jake's hands as if she were handing him a plate of food.

"Wow," Jake said, looking at the beautifully engraved title, feeling the aged maroon leather that covered the book. "That's quite a title."

"It was quite a place," Ginny said, smiling with a nod.

Jake glanced at her peculiarly. She stopped smiling and put her eyes down.

Jake walked over to a table, then began turning pages. He suddenly stopped on an article from a newspaper, so condensed it was difficult to read. The headline read, "Fire Destroys Volstead Brothel. Two Women Perish."

Jake squinted. He tried to read the print, but it was too small. He turned to find Ginny, who was leaning over his shoulder. "Oh, Ginny. Can we look up this article in the archives?" He pointed.

"What is that date?"

"Um, February 23rd, 1864."

"Oh, that was a long time ago, Mr. Butterfield. I have my doubts."

"Can we maybe try?"

Ginny considered him momentarily, rocked on her shoes and cane, then said, "Sure we can. Follow me."

She walked over to a microfiche catalog and began rummaging through. Eventually, she pulled out a pack of slides and went to a machine. She put her eyes to the holder and began to page through. Jake waited impatiently. Finally, she said, "Here it is."

"Can you print it?"

"Yes, just a minute." She printed the page, then said, "We just got this new printer. It's amazing. Hold it," she added. "It continues on another page. Oh, look here. I will print this too. And there is another article about one of the ladies. I'll print this one too."

She printed all three articles and handed them to Jake.

Jake shuffled them, looking at the titles of each. His heart raced. He went over to the table, sat down, and started to read.

Fire Destroys Volstead Brothel. Two Women Perish.

Last night a fire engulfed the Volstead Brothel. The fire began in the bar and raced upstairs. The Sandusky Volunteer Fire Brigade battled the blaze for over two hours before finally extinguishing it.

Most of the women and patrons inside made it out. Unfortunately, two women perished. Big Rosie McGinnis, age 56, lost her life, along with Marie Butterfield, age 23. Witnesses say that Big Rosie had made it safely out of the fire but upon finding out that one of her girls had not made it out safely, she raced back inside to try and find her.

Jake put down the article, dumbfounded.

His palms felt moist, and beads of sweat formed on his forehead.

His mind was telling him that it could not be true, but in his heart, he knew better.

It was true.

It was all true, and he began to remember all the encounters, all the conversations he'd had with the two ladies. How odd they had been, how they dressed in such old clothing. He gasped. The mirror… Now he understood. He should have seen their reflections as they were sitting by the Christmas tree.

His heart was racing like never before as he pulled up the other two articles. The first was about Big Rosie.

Big Rosie Was Well Liked

Rosie McGinnis, known affectionately as Big Rosie, owned and ruled the Volstead Brothel for over 25 years. In those years, she became an endearing as well as controversial figure to many in the town of Sandusky. The controversy and mystery surrounding her life began shortly after she arrived in town. She purchased the brothel from a private group of businessmen who remained anonymous. Rosie set out to reform the place, claiming that her "ladies" deserved to be treated like ladies, a claim that was met with a scoff from many in the community, who maintained that ladies would not be working in a brothel. But Rosie kept true to her word, cleaning up troublesome clientele and raising pay, and much to the surprise of many, the brothel gained somewhat of a respectable, though sordid, reputation.

Rosie's past cast a shadow over her lively character. In her past she lived in Louisville, and there, she had been accused of murdering her husband. According to some documents, she shot him on a winter night in 1843. She claimed it was self-defense, that he had been drinking and had tried to kill her. A jury that was split for several days finally found her innocent. Thereafter, she moved to Sandusky for a fresh start. But news of her past traveled with her and marred her reputation. Despite all this, one thing is for certain: Big Rosie will be greatly missed.

Marie Butterfield, Little Is Known.

Little is known of the young woman who perished in the fire, other than she was the wife of Captain Bradley Butterfield, who went missing during the Battle of Gettysburg last July and has not been heard from since. It is not known why or when Mrs. Butterfield began to work at the brothel, but rumor has it she lost a child, left her home in the countryside, and ended up at the Volstead.

Mrs. Butterfield was 23 years old when she perished.

Jake sat at the table, staring blankly out the window in front of him. His head was spinning. He was piecing it all together...almost. Could there have been someone else named Big Rosie? It could be a common nickname. No. No, something was going on. And somehow, he had been brought into this mystery.

But why?

Why was he smack dab in the middle of it? And why could he see them? Then again, Ginny and Father Tom could see them. The people at church had seemed to notice Big Rosie nodding at them during the Sign of Peace, or did they? He himself had seen Big Rosie exchange glances and greetings with people as they left the church. But he never saw them speak to each other. And why hadn't Sal ever alluded to either of them?

"Jake?" The voice startled him. He looked up. It was Father Tom.

"Jake, are you all finished? I have to lock up."

Jake shook his head slowly, his mouth open, staring down at the articles in front of him. He looked up at Father Tom. "Father, how long have you known Big Rosie?"

"Oh, a long time now. It's been a number of years. Why, is something wrong?"

"It's… well… I…" He glanced at the articles, then looked up. Was he losing his mind? He needed to think this through. "Never mind, Father Tom. Thank you for letting me in."

Jake scooped up the articles, folded them, and put them in his jacket pocket.

The two men walked to the door. As Jake stepped outside, Father Tom said, "Oh, Jake. I almost forgot. There was one more letter in the box you were looking through yesterday. Ginny told me they just cataloged it, she found it on the shelf, and she thought it might interest you."

Jake exhaled loudly, shaking his head, wondering what else he could possibly find. He took the letter and left.

~ ~ ~ ~

Jake trembled as he walked down the street. It was nearly mid-morning. Snow was falling, and the streets were quiet, almost as quiet as they had been only a week earlier. It was Christmas morning, and everyone was at home. Jake walked up the alley to the back door of the Volstead and went up the back staircase that led to his room. He passed Frannie's room, pausing, thinking. Then he went into his room and sat on his bed, stretching out his legs. He pulled out the articles and read them a second time. Then he unfolded the last letter, the one Father Tom had given him, and began to read.

His eyes widened, and he set the letter down on his lap, glancing out the window, thinking. He picked it up again, looking at the date on the letter. It was dated the day after the fire. He quickly checked the articles to be sure. Yes, the letter had been written the day after the two women died.

It was from Captain Butterfield.

Jake knew what he had to do.

He refolded the letter and went down the hall to Big Rosie's room. He could feel his heart racing and his spine tingling as he carried the letter in front of him as if it were a king's crown. He walked down the hall bravely, egged on by the realization that he must have been chosen for this moment. Somehow, in time, he had been chosen.

He reached Big Rosie's door and listened, then slowly raised his hand and knocked.

He heard her footsteps cross the floor, and then she opened the door and smiled. "Good morning, Mr. Butterfield. Merry Christmas to you."

Jake gazed at her, marveling at the reality of the person standing before him. "Merry Christmas to you too, Rosie."

"Would you like to come in?"

"No, I shouldn't. Big Rosie...I mean, Rosie. I have something I wanted to show you."

"What is it?"

Jake swallowed. "It's a letter...that Captain Butterfield wrote to his wife the day after she died.

"Where did you get this?" Big Rosie asked, her brow arching into a furrow.

"It was in the papers from the house I inherited." He extended the letter toward Rosie.

She looked at his shaking hand with a disbelieving glare. Then she took the letter and looked down at it.

Jake said, "I think you should read it."

She glanced up at him, with a cross look on her face, then unfolded the letter. Her eyes drifted to and fro and gently down the page. Her face changed from an expression of distrust to one of intrigue, then to one of compassion. When she finished, she wiped a tear from her eye and stayed still for several moments, looking blankly at the signature.

Jake said, "Will you show this to Frannie?"

Big Rosie nodded, "I will. I will, Mr. Butterfield."

Jake said, "I have to go now... Rosie."

Big Rosie extended her right hand. "It was a pleasure to meet you, Mr. Butterfield."

Jake smiled. "It was the same for me, Rosie. Merry Christmas."

"Aye," she said, smiling, and closed the door.

Jake stood there in silence. He realized he had been practically holding his breath the whole time. He was in shock, and in awe, and yet, he was not afraid. He slowly turned and went back to his room.

He lay on his bed, breathing deeply, thinking about everything. He would be leaving in the morning, going back to Louisville — somewhere in Louisville, at least. He only had to go to the attorney's office to close the sale of the property and pick up the check. He went over to his bed and lay down, wondering about it all and waiting for time to pass.

~ ~ ~ ~

Frannie opened the door of her room to see Big Rosie standing there with a peculiar look on her face.

"Merry Christmas, Rosie," Frannie said, cheerfully.

"Aye, to you too. Frannie, I have something to tell ye. They don't need us here anymore. We can both go home now."

Frannie clutched her hands to her chest. "Why, I can't leave, Rosie. I have nowhere to go."

"Yes, you do have somewhere to go, Frannie. You can go home now."

"No!" Frannie said, glancing at the drawer where his picture was. "You were there, Rosie. You heard him. You saw the look on his face. He said he would never forgive me."

"Aye, Frannie, but I don't think it's true anymore."

"It is true, Rosie. It will always be true. I remember the day so clearly." Frannie stood frozen. Her memory drifted back to the day. The day her sorrow fell upon her.

It had been a cold morning. She had just finished cleaning the bars and kitchen area. There was a knock at the door, but all the girls were asleep from their late night the night before. Even Big Rosie was still asleep.

Frannie walked cheerfully to the door and opened it.

There he was, the love of her life, staring back at her with a look of disdain on his face.

"How could you!" he demanded. His anger scared her.

"Oh, my… Oh, my God." Her breathing began to labor, and she squeezed her chest. "You're…you're alive…. Oh, my God. Oh, Brad."

"Don't you dare say anything to me. I will never forgive you."

Frannie suddenly realized what he was thinking, and her eyes widened in horror. "No, Brad, you don't… I am not…"

"Who is it, Frannie?" Big Rosie loudly called from upstairs.

Frannie turned with her eyes wide. "Rosie, please come down…"

She turned. Brad had turned away and was walking to his horse. "Brad!" she screamed, running after him, tripping on her apron. "Brad!"

He turned, gave her one final glare, then kicked his horse, yelling loudly, "Go!"

Frannie stood in the mud of the street, shouting, "Brad, please...Brad!"

Big Rosie ran out. "Frannie, what is it?"

She cried out, tears streaming down her face as she began to hyperventilate. "Oh, Rosie, I have to go after him. He... he... he said he would never forgive me. He thinks I am one of the ladies..."

Rosie took Frannie into her arms and hugged her. Then she stood, watching Frannie's husband gallop out of town.

Frannie screamed, "I have to go, Rosie! He doesn't understand!"

Rosie pulled Frannie toward the house. "Let him cool down, Frannie. Tomorrow you can go out to the house. I will go with you, and we will explain everything."

"I have to talk to him, Rosie. He thinks I am one of the ladies."

"Don't worry, Frannie. I'll set everything straight. Don't you mind it another minute."

"Oh, Rosie. I'm scared. He said he would never forgive me."

"People say things they don't mean, especially when they are angry. Now, come inside."

Frannie remembered coming inside.

She had never left since.

Rosie interrupted her thoughts, "We can go now, Frannie," Rosie said, gently reaching out her hand.

Frannie buried her face in her hands, then looked up. "He said he'd never forgive me." She buried her face back in her hands and wept.

Rosie said sternly, "Frannie, you need to trust me right now. Get your coat. I have someplace I need you to see."

Frannie hesitated, glancing at the door.

Rosie looked down at her sternly, saying, "Now, grab your coat and put on your shoes."

Frannie nervously complied, and she followed Rosie out of the room and down the back steps.

~ ~ ~ ~

When Frannie stepped outside, the air hit her face, causing her spine to tingle. She had not felt a rush of air like this in a long time. There was an inch of freshly fallen snow in the alley. Frannie watched Rosie hurry ahead of her and down the alley. Then she noticed something strange: Rosie was walking so lightly that she was not making any tracks in the snow. Frannie looked behind herself and noticed no footprints. She thought that odd, but she kept following.

They walked to the main street and out toward the country. They passed stores Frannie had never seen and lights she had never fathomed. There were new homes and buildings in places where Frannie remembered there to be farmhouses and large fields. Before long, they turned down a country road that Frannie recognized. There was a sign she had never seen before but whose words she had heard a hundred times: Old Railroad Road.

Frannie stopped in the middle of the road in front of a house up on a gentle sloping hill. "Hold it, Rosie, wait. Where are we?"

"You don't recognize this place, Frannie?"

Frannie knew the house. It was her house. But it had changed.

It was still wood-sided, but the once-vibrant green paint was gone, replaced by a light blue paint that was peeling everywhere. The wide stone steps, now tarnished and moss-covered, were the same steps Brad had carried her up when he brought her home from Detroit as his new bride. They were the same wide steps she had kissed him on before he left for war. They were the same wide steps she had carried her infant son's body down to his little grave in the graveyard. It hit her all at once. The graveyard. Kyle was buried there.

Every night at sunset, from her upstairs room at the Volstead, she had looked out the window in this direction—thousands of times. At first, she had known that her little one was buried here, but as time passed, her memory faded, and eventually she looked out the window knowing part of her was here, but she had been unable to remember exactly what part.

She glanced to the right. Up the hill, away from the house, was the graveyard.

Frannie turned to Rosie. "My baby is buried up there."

"Aye, Frannie, aye. Let's go up and have a look."

Frannie took Rosie's hand, steadying herself as they walked up the snow-covered hill. They entered the small family cemetery and walked over to the three nearest graves, which all sat next to each other in a small group, covered with snow.

Frannie glanced at the gravestones, then looked back toward the house. The wooden screen door was flapping in the wind. The whole place and its grounds seemed abandoned.

Frannie looked at Rosie, her eyes asking for help. Rosie nodded toward the gravestones. Frannie looked down, focusing her attention on them. She stepped forward and brushed the snow away from the first stone. She began to read as a warm tear cascaded down her cold cheek.

Kyle Butterfield
Infant Son
Born March 7, 1863
Died December 3, 1863

She saw how old the first stone was. She was the one who had purchased it when Kyle died. She stepped to the next one, though she didn't remember another stone next to Kyle's. She brushed the snow away.

Captain Bradley Butterfield
Husband
Born July 5, 1839
Died February 24, 1864

Frannie fell to her knees in the snow. "He died? My Bradley died?" Tears began to flow more strongly now. "But how? When?" she asked, looking up at Rosie.

"It's okay, Frannie. It's all going to be okay."

Frannie looked up at her, her expression helpless. Rosie smiled warmly, trying to reassure her.

Frannie glanced at the next stone, then moved over to it. She leaned forward and brushed away the snow. She straightened up and began to read.

Marie Francis Butterfield
"Frannie"
Wife
Born January 7, 1840
Died February 23, 1864
My dear wife, I will always love you

Frannie put her face in her cold hands, then pulled them away and examined them. "Rosie, am I... Am I really...dead?"

Rosie bent down and helped her to stand. Then she hugged her. "Yes. We both are Frannie, but it's okay. We're standing here, aren't we? Look there, how much Bradley loved you. Look what he wrote on your gravestone."

"But...but what happened, Rosie? I don't remember... I don't remember anymore."

"Frannie, there was a fire the night Bradley came to see you. All the girls got out, and I did too. But when we were outside, I didn't see you, and I realized you were sleeping in the basement. I ran in to save you, and…"

"And what, Rosie?" Frannie asked, her moist eyes glistening wide. "What happened?"

"I made it to your room in the basement, but when I opened the door and saw you lying on the bed, I… I stepped toward you…and the floor above us collapsed. We died in the fire, Frannie."

Frannie looked down at her hands and her dress. She felt her face, her lips. Her face grew confused, as if she were thinking. And then she looked up in realization.

"Why did we stay here?"

"Frannie, when a person dies with great regret, it can trap them. You regretted coming to the Volstead…and somehow, you were stuck. You didn't want to leave."

"But why did you stay?"

"Frannie, I stayed because of you. I was not going to leave you behind. Besides." Rosie lowered her glance. "I feel it was my fault, Frannie. I stopped you from going to see Brad that day. I told you to wait until the morning. I regret it so much." Rosie turned away as a tear fell down her cheek.

Frannie glanced back, scanning all three stones. Her family torn apart by the war, by the death of their baby Kyle, and then the misunderstanding between them. It was all overwhelming her. Seeing all three graves next to each other made it seem like none of it ever happened. It made it seem like they'd shared a life together and were buried together in the same cemetery when they died, like everyone else. She wiped her eyes, trying to understand why she was there and what it meant for her.

She looked at her grave again, unable to contain her emotions. There it was. The date she died. The day Brad came to see her.

Frannie closed her eyes in sorrow, remembering. Then her eyes burst open, and she glanced back at the gravestone in the middle. She turned to Rosie, "Rosie, he died the day after I did?"

Rosie nodded. "He could not bear losing you, Frannie. He took his own life the next day."

"He did?" Frannie asked, her voice trailing off. Her eyes suddenly filled with worry.

"But first, he wrote you a letter."

Frannie looked up. "He did what?"

"Here," Rosie said, handing her a piece of parchment.

Frannie wiped the tears from her eyes, then wiped her hands on her blouse sleeves, drying them before taking the letter. Her hands trembled as she looked down at it, then up at Rosie with a worried look.

Big Rosie nodded, wearing the confident, tight-lipped smile she always had when she gave advice.

Frannie unfolded it carefully. She recognized his handwriting. She began to read in earnest.

My Dear Frannie,

I know you are in Heaven because there could be no other place for you.

I heard the news today. It has broken my heart into a thousand pieces. I would have known the truth if only I had taken the time to listen to you. Instead of chastising you, I could have taken you into my arms and hugged you tighter than I ever did before.

Now you are gone from this world. Your life is over…and mine is too.

News of the fire reached me at noon. I ran to the site and was told that the proprietor, Big Rosie, and you had perished. Frannie, my heart ached for you. Then I overheard someone talking. They said that you were not one of the brothel ladies, just someone who stayed on to help Big Rosie cook and clean. I now understand that you had no other means to survive.

Frannie, it didn't matter. I will always love you. Always. And I will never love anyone else.

I will not be long in this world because I do not deserve to be. You died not knowing that I love you. My hope is to join you if you will have me.

I pray this letter will reach Heaven so that you can see my heart.

Love always,
Bradley

Frannie looked up. "He said he couldn't live without me... and he took his own life?"

Big Rosie nodded.

Frannie closed her eyes and dropped her head back, breathing harder than ever. She held the letter to her heart as the tears fell. "I didn't know, Rosie. I didn't know."

"Neither did I, Frannie."

"Where did you get this?"

"Jake Butterfield gave it to me. Somehow, he figured it all out. Brad was his great-great-uncle."

Frannie nodded. She understood.

Big Rosie smiled. "You can go home now, Frannie."

"To where, Rosie? Everyone I loved is dead."

Rosie waved her hand in the air. She drew a wide circle in front of them with her finger, and the cold day was cut through to an opening in a parallel world. Rosie stepped into the circle and reached for Frannie to take her hand. Frannie took her by the hand, and they stepped through the circle onto a soft, lightly snow-covered field. It seemed they were standing in the same spot, but here it was not cold nor windy. There were no gravestones in the ground in front of them either. Frannie looked behind her, into the very snow-covered day they had stepped out of.

Rosie said, "Not there, Frannie. Look over here."

Frannie turned. In the distance was the two-story farmhouse with the wide front porch. But it was not rundown. Birds were chirping loudly even though it was winter. The sun shone brightly, glistening on the snow-covered front porch swing as it stirred slowly in the gentle, cool wind.

Frannie turned to Rosie, her eyes questioning. "Rosie, is it all real?"

"It is real, Frannie," Rosie said, wiping a tear from her eye. Then she pointed. "Look."

Frannie looked on as the wooden screen door opened with its old familiar squeak. Out stepped Bradley, with his blonde hair lying neatly to the side, his broad shoulders strong as ever. He glanced over his shoulder for a moment, then let the door close gently, as if he were trying to keep quiet.

He turned toward Frannie. His face beamed as he ran down the steps and across the snow-covered grass, shouting, "Frannie!"

Frannie started for him then hesitated, unsure of herself and what they had never said to each other. "Oh, Brad, I'm sor—"

He reached her before she could finish. He lifted his finger and shook his head, his eyes conveying deep sorrow. "No, Frannie. You have nothing to be sorry for. I am sorry!"

He took her into his arms, kissed her slowly, and then pulled back to look at her. She saw the truth of it all in his eyes. He did truly love her. He did understand.

He took Frannie by the hand. "Come with me. I have someone who wants to see you."

Frannie walked with him up the stairs and into her home. The air was fresh and breezy, and the wallpaper and furniture were just as she remembered them, only newer. A fire was going in the fireplace, and a Christmas tree was next to it near the window. On the other side of the fireplace was a bassinet. Frannie looked to Brad and covered her mouth in disbelief. "Kyle?"

"Yes, he's been waiting for you. We have both been waiting for you. This is our second chance, Frannie, the chance we never got before."

Frannie's eyes closed as her breathing labored. She remembered the last time she held her little baby's limp body in her arms on the day he died. She walked over hesitantly and cautiously peered down at his sleeping body.

Brad whispered, "You can wake him."

"No, no," Frannie said, looking up, her face and eyes glistening with tears of joy. "Let him sleep. I will be here when he wakes up."

They turned and stepped back into the center of the room. Frannie wiped the tears from her eyes. "Oh, Brad. We are alive again."

"Yes, Frannie. We are here in Heaven. This is our home."

She reached up, placing her arms over his broad shoulders, and said, "I will always love you, Bradley Butterfield."

"And I you, Marie Francis Butterfield."

They kissed warmly.

Frannie's eyes widened. "Wait, I have to get Rosie."

She ran outside and shouted, "Rosie!"

Rosie had turned back toward the circle that led to the snow-covered day of the old world they had stepped out of. She turned back to Frannie, half smiling.

"Where are you going?" Frannie shouted. "Stay here!"

"I will be back, Frannie. I have something to take care of."

"No, Rosie. I need you!"

Rosie stopped one more time. "Don't worry, Frannie. It will be okay."

Frannie watched Rosie step back through the swirling circle that had brought her here. Then the circle in the air closed up, and she was gone.

~ ~ ~ ~

Jake startled awake.

He must have fallen asleep.

He got up, went down to Big Rosie's room.

The door was ajar.

He opened the door slowly. Before him was a completely empty room with nothing but a broad old wooden floor and one wooden chair. He walked in, looking to where the curtains had been, where the table had been, and where the Christmas tree had been. All of it was gone. A shiver went up his spine.

He backed out of the room and ran down the hall to Frannie's room. As he opened the door, he already knew what he would find. Nothing. It was barren, like Rosie's room, except for an old bed and a dresser with the top drawer slightly open. Jake walked over and nervously peered into the drawer. There was something there—an old photograph turned upside down. He picked it up and examined it. His mouth dropped open.

It was Captain Bradley Butterfield, standing proudly in his Union soldier's uniform. Next to him, clutching his arm and wearing a pretty white dress, was Frannie. Jake closed his eyes. It was all becoming clear now. All the letters. All the conversations. Frannie being so timid, Rosie... Rosie. Why was she here?

He held the photo to his chest, breathing slowly, taking it all in, grateful he had somehow been a part of whatever was happening.

He went back to his room, tucked the picture away with his papers, picked up his coat, and went out for a walk. It had all been for a reason. He had been chosen, and it had all been true. The picture in his hand proved it.

Monday

As soon as the sun was well up on Monday, Mr. Bixby got out of bed, dressed and hustled over to the Volstead. When he reached the back door, he noticed it was ajar. A bad sign.

He went up the back stairway and came to Frannie's room. He peered in. It was empty. A scowl began to grow on his face. He went to Jake's room and looked in. It too, was empty. "Argghh!" he shouted, with clenched fist.

Finally, he went to Rosie's room. He already knew what he would find. It was completely empty. Because he could not come out on Christmas Eve or Christmas Day, he had missed his chance to stop everything. He clenched his teeth, writhing in pain, then walked in, picked up a chair, and threw it across the room. Rosie and Frannie had escaped his imprisonment. The ones in charge of hell would try to make him pay for this. He was not worried though. He would lie his way out of it.

He thought to the day he had made this deal. He would be allowed out of the Dark Prison, on one condition. He had to promise souls, lots of them. He had done well, delivering over a thousand in a little less than 100 years. But the powers that be did not count by victories, they counted by failures, and now Rosie would be considered one of his failures.

Stuck souls always presented a problem for the Dark Angels. Just like the Angels on the good side, once assigned, they had to see them through. It was like almost winning the race and having everyone stop at the finish line, refusing to cross the line. This, of course, meant they still had time to change their minds.

Long ago, his plan was to sweep Big Rosie, and her brothel ladies into a tragic, unforeseen death. Souls living immoral lives, dying tragically, had the best chance of being denied entry to Heaven, at least for a long time, and in some cases, forever. He had helped Olga get drunk enough to start the fire. He helped her leave out the back door, so the blame would be fixed upon her. But someone else had woken the girls up. Someone else had gotten them all out of the fire. That was his first failure: not noticing that someone was around who might do such a thing. He suspected it was Father Tom.

But even after the blaze was set, and even after they all escaped, there was still hope, for Rosie had run back in. At least, he thought, he had gotten one soul. But then Rosie found a reason to stay, a reason based on love, because Frannie was innocent. That act of love allowed Rosie to "not cross" the finish line. She managed to pause her entry into the eternal realm where her judgment would have taken place.

He kicked the tipped over chair, and walked further into Rosie's expansive, empty room. It felt strange, knowing she had been in the sort of purgatory for so long, and now all traces were gone. Then he saw it. Over on the windowsill, was a small blue ribbon in the shape of a cross and a piece of paper. He went over and picked it up. This had belonged to Olga. He read the words. 'Help"

He looked out the window, his eyes ablaze. He had been looking for Olga for a very long time.

~ ~ ~ ~

Rosie pulled open the old wooden door and walked into St. Mary's. The church was illuminated by the sunshine streaming in through the southern-facing stained-glass windows. It was empty inside. She dipped her hand in the holy water and blessed herself, feeling the old, familiar shiver run up her spine. She was glad she was alone. She felt more at home here than anywhere else, and she had for a long time. She walked up the center aisle lightly and slowly, trying not to make too much noise with her thick-heeled shoes.

She reached the front and looked up at Jesus hanging on the cross. She blessed herself again, making the Sign of the Cross, then turned to kneel.

Suddenly, the front door of the church creaked open. Rosie turned to see who it was, then smiled. It was Father Tom.

"Rosie," he said, looking relieved as he began to walk toward her. "I'm glad you're okay." When he reached her, he stood a few feet away, with his arms crossed, smiling.

"Hello, Father Tom," Rosie said. "And were ye worried about me?"

He dropped his arms, opened his hands, and exclaimed, "I didn't know where you went."

Rosie stood up to face him, and said, "Well... I had to take Frannie home."

"I know. I know you did." He paused, thinking. Then he asked, "Aren't you coming home too?"

She turned away and looked down. "I am afraid to, Father." She kept her gaze on the floor.

"I see," Father Tom said. "You don't have to be, Rosie. I've told you."

"But I've done so much, Father. I hurt many people with my schemes to make money in my past."

"Now, Rosie. We've talked about this many times. Look right up there." He pointed to the cross. "You're sorry for what you did. Are you not?"

"I am, Father. I truly am."

"It's all been forgiven, Rosie. Somewhere it says, 'love cast out a multitude of sins.' Look what you did for Frannie. Not leaving her."

She paused. "Are you really a priest, Father?"

Father Tom smiled. "Not really, Rosie."

"Then what are ye?"

He smiled again. "I'm an Angel."

"Ah, go on now. Are ye kidding me?"

"Rosie, don't you remember the day I took you by the hand, pulled you from the fire, and started taking you up to Heaven?"

"Oh, my," Rosie said. "That was you? I had forgotten."

"Do you remember what you told me?"

"I do, Father," she said.

Father Tom smiled. "You told me you would not leave Frannie behind. You told me to go away and come back another time. It was a great act of courage and love, Rosie. Had you not protected Frannie, she may have fallen prey to the influence of the Dark Side"

Rosie wiped her tear away as a small smile came over her face. "I'm glad I did, Father."

Father Tom smiled again. "I'm glad you did too, Rosie."

Rosie nodded. Then she looked up suddenly and asked, "Ginny too?"

Father Tom's smile widened. "Yes, Ginny is an Angel too. I'm her boss."

"And ye both were here trying to help me?"

"Well, you were trying to help Frannie. The least we could do was try to help you. Besides, you were my assignment. All Angels have to see their assignments through. It's the rule."

Rosie began to shake her head. "I should have known." Then she looked up, her smile fading quickly, and asked sternly, "Who is Mr. Bixby?"

Father Tom felt his own smile fall away. "He is an Angel too, Rosie, but he is with the Dark Side."

"I knew there was something dark about him. Now it makes sense." She paused, staring at the floor, thinking back to the day before the fire. Mr. Bixby had been there. He had been around the Volstead for about two weeks before the fire, spending time with Olga. She had looked troubled, but Rosie had thought nothing of it. Now, though, it all made sense. Olga's message made sense. She too, like Frannie, must be stuck.

Rosie looked up at Father Tom, realizing he was watching her.

He extended his hand. "Well, enough about all that, Rosie. Are you ready to go?"

"Well, I… First, I have a question, Father."

Father Tom sighed. "What is it this time, Rosie?"

"You Angels have to listen to us humans, right? I mean, you're not in charge of us, right?"

Father Tom, sighed again, furrowing his brow. "Yes, that is true. You have Free Will. May I ask why you are asking?"

Big Rosie smiled. "Well, Father, I can't leave just yet. I have something else I have to do; someone I need to help."

Father Tom tightened his lip. "Rosie, you can't just—"

"Ah! Father, now, I can do what I like! You just said I could, did you not?"

"Where are you going?" he asked, a bit exasperated.

She looked off into the distance. "There is a girl who was in dark trouble here in Sandusky long ago. I heard from her recently. I need to go see about her. I have a feeling she is still in that trouble."

"Who?"

"Olga," Rosie said.

Father Tom swallowed, then nodded.

"Don't go far, Father. I may need your help on that one too."

"My help?" He looked up toward Heaven, then back down. "Will you be needing Ginny's help too?"

"Aye," Rosie said. "I might need her as well."

Rosie turned and walked briskly down the church's center aisle, but before she reached the front door, she turned back. "I'll see ye soon, Father."

Father Tom waved. "See you soon, Rosie."

~ ~ ~ ~

A little after 10:00 a.m., Jake strolled down the main street in Sandusky with a broad smile on his face. After an early breakfast at the Port Sandusky Restaurant, where he had said goodbye to Don and Sherri, he had gone to the attorney's office to wrap things up. A brand-new life was indeed in front of him. His car was packed with all his things, just as it had been when he'd arrived only a week earlier.

He drove back to the Volstead, where Sal would be opening up. He went to the door and found it unlocked.

Sal had his back to the door, with his hat turned backward, fumbling with a bottle of something. He turned. "Well, I'll be a monkey's uncle. Jake Butterfield!"

Jake laughed. "Hi, Sal. I had to come and say goodbye." He pulled up to his favorite barstool.

Sal looked at the bottle in his hands, the one he could not open. He grimaced and set it aside. He turned his hat around frontward.

Jake asked, "Can I get a coffee and a ham sandwich for the road, old boy?"

"You sure can, Jake. You sure can." Sal flipped his hat around backward and ducked into the kitchen, saying, "Coming right up."

Moments later, Sal returned. He took off his bar apron, came around the Jake's side of the bar, and sat on the barstool next to Jake. "Well, Jake. It has been a pleasure to meet you. We're going to miss you around here. You've become one of us."

Jake smiled. "Well, you may not be able to get rid of me that easy, Sal."

"What do you mean?"

"I didn't sell the old house."

Sal's eyes widened. "Well, I'll be a monkey's uncle. Why not?"

"Well, you know, I kind of like the place, and there is a lot of history there. I think it will be a good place for me to do some writing."

"So, you plan on doing some writing?"

"Actually, I have a great story to tell."

"What's it about?"

"It's about this place, and two trapped souls who find their way home. I may even be able to slide you into the story."

"Well, Jake, that is fantastic. I like it. Are you leaving town today?"

"Yes, I have to go back to Louisville. I want to try to work things out with my wife."

Sal smiled, nodding. "Well, I'll be... I'm proud of you, Jake."

Jake stood and shook Sal's hand heartily, his face beaming. "See ya soon, Sal."

"See ya soon, Jake."

As Jake headed for the door, Sal called out, "Hey, Jake, what are you going to call that book?"

"I'm going to call it *Home for Christmas*."

"I like that, Jake. That's good. That's real good."

The end?

We have a feeling this is just the beginning.

Final Things
Could you rate this book with on Amazon?

Review on Amazon
To find me on amazon, search DP Conway books.

Sign Up for my Monthly Newsletter at
dpconway.com
I promise not to annoy you.

Drawing from his Irish American heritage, D.P. Conway weaves faith and hope into his storytelling, exploring the profound mysteries of life and its connection to the Angels and the rest of the unseen Eternal World. His works consistently convey the triumph of light over darkness, inspiring readers to find strength and solace amidst life's trials.

Also by D. P. Conway

Stand Alone Novels
Las Vegas Down
Parkland
The Wancheen
Marisella

The Christmas Collection
Starry Night
The Ghost of Christmas to Come
Nava
Twelve Days
Home for Christmas

Coming Soon
Mary Queen of Hearts
And hopefully many, many, more….

Afterlife Chronicles: Angel Sagas Series
The Epic Series based on Genesis and Revelation
Dawn of Days
Rebellion
Judgment
Empire
The Innocents
And 7 more titles in this epic series.

See many more of D.P. Conway's books on Amazon or visit
www.dpconway.com

Copyright & Publication

Daylights Publishing
5498 Dorothy Drive Suite 3:16
Cleveland, OH 44070

www.dpconway.com
www.daylightspublishing.com

Photo sources and credits are listed at www.dpconway.com

Cover: Nate Myers, Colleen Conway Cooper
Developmental Editor: Colleen Conway Cooper
Developmental Editor 2: Caroline Knecht
Copy Editor: Connie Swenson
Proof Reader: Marisa DiRuggiero Conway
Narrator: Steve Corona